"Go to bed, Kate."

Drew's voice was hardly more than a whisper.

"Come with me."

It was a siren's call, the words stroking over him with an almost physical touch. Drew clenched his hands into fists, trying to remember all the reasons he couldn't do what she was asking.

"You're upset," he managed finally. "You're not thinking clearly."

"I'm thinking clearly for the first time in days." Her voice trembled but her words didn't falter. "I'm tired of pretending, Drew. Pretending that I don't want you. Pretending that you don't want me."

Drew stared down at her, telling himself that he was going to walk away, that this wasn't going to go any further. "This is wrong. I'm supposed to be protecting you."

"Then," she said, reaching out to him, "you shouldn't let me out of your sight."

ABOUT THE AUTHOR

Dallas Schulze is a full-time writer who lives in Southern California with her husband and calico cat. An avid reader, she devours books by the boxful. To indulge her love of the American West, Dallas is a docent at a local museum dedicated to the period. In what little spare time she has, she enjoys doll collecting, old radio shows, classic and current movies, doll making, sewing, quilting and baking. Several of Dallas's novels have been finalists in the RITA awards for outstanding romance fiction.

Books by Dallas Schulze

HARLEQUIN AMERICAN ROMANCE

Don't miss any of our special offers. Write to us at the following address for information on our newest releases.

Harlequin Reader Service
P.O. Box 1397, Buffalo, NY 14240
Canadian address: P.O. Box 603,
Fort Erie, Ont. L2A 5X3

DALLAS SCHULZE

STRONG ARMS OF THE LAW

Harlequin Books

TORONTO • NEW YORK • LONDON
AMSTERDAM • PARIS • SYDNEY • HAMBURG
STOCKHOLM • ATHENS • TOKYO • MILAN
MADRID • WARSAW • BUDAPEST • AUCKLAND

Published May 1993

ISBN 0-373-16486-6

STRONG ARMS OF THE LAW

Chapter One

"I don't want this assignment." Drew Hunter crossed the small office and tossed a thin folder onto the cluttered desk.

The man behind the desk didn't immediately acknowledge Drew's presence. For several slow heartbeats there was not a sound in the room. Drew waited. He knew Lavery had heard him and would respond in his own sweet time.

The room was small and dark despite the edgy light provided by the fluorescent fixture overhead. The two men were at once very different and very much alike. Physically, there were few similarities. One was swarthy, with dark eyes and a thin, lanky build. The other was lightly tanned with eyes of vivid, icy blue and a leanly muscled frame. But beneath the surface, they shared a belief that one should walk alone through life, observing but seldom participating on any personal level. It made them good cops, but poor candidates for emotional involvement.

Martin Lavery finished reading the report in front of him and set it aside before reaching for the file Drew had tossed down. He pulled it across the desk and flipped it open. It wasn't necessary for him to refresh his memory on its contents, and both men knew it. Lavery never hurried anything. After looking at it for a moment, he closed the folder and lifted his eyes to Drew's face.

"Why are you here, Hunter?" The voice was as deep and slow moving as the man to whom it belonged.

"I don't want this assignment, Lieutenant." Only someone who knew him well could have heard the underlying tension in Drew's voice. Lavery knew him very well.

"Why?"

"I'm a cop. Not a baby-sitter."

"Ms. Sloane needs our protection."

"She needs a baby-sitter. I'm not it." Drew shifted his stance, his face tightening as he put weight on his left leg.

"Sit down, Hunter. How is your leg?"

Drew remained standing. "My leg is fine. If that's why you're giving me this job, you can give it to someone else. I'm ready to go back to work."

"Sit down," Lavery said again. "You don't have to prove how tough you are in here."

Drew hesitated a moment longer and then sank into the hard chair next to him. He stretched his leg out in front of him, but other than that he refused to acknowledge the ache that had settled in his thigh.

"How is your leg?" Lavery asked again, a subtle softening in his tone that reminded Drew that they'd worked together a long time. If there was anyone who could say he truly knew him, it was Martin Lavery.

"It hurts like hell sometimes," he admitted. "But I can handle it. I'm ready for a real assignment, Martin. I don't need any more rest cures."

Lavery's dark eyes studied the other man, noting the lines of pain that bracketed his mouth, the hollows under his pale blue eyes that made it clear he wasn't sleeping. He knew it wasn't physical pain that was keeping Drew up nights. The fact that his partner had died in the same incident that had left him wounded was eating into his guts like acid. That, like the wound in his leg, was something only time could heal.

Lavery offered no words of sympathy. They had known each other long enough for the words to be unnecessary. He returned his attention to the file. The edge of a photo showed beneath the official reports and he pulled the picture out to lay it on top of the paperwork.

"An attractive woman," he commented, studying the photo.

Drew said nothing, and Lavery leaned back in his chair, steepling his fingers beneath his chin as he studied the younger man. "You've done this kind of work before. What's the problem this time?"

"I don't need any more rest. I've been sitting behind a desk for the past three months. I need something to sink my teeth into."

"Like Lester Davis?" Lavery asked softly.

A muscle twitched in Drew's jaw, confirming the accuracy of his superior's guess. Lavery looked back down at the report, tapping one long finger on the photograph.

"Kate Sloane stuck her neck out in coming to us. We're asking her to stick it out a lot farther by testifying. I don't think she knows just how far out. We've been trying to get a solid case on Davis for almost five years. For the first time, we've got enough on him to take it to court. I'd think you'd want to be in on this."

Drew stirred restlessly. Of course he wanted to see Davis fall. He had more reason than most to want the man brought to his knees. But this assignment... He glanced at the photo and then looked away, unable to explain his reluctance, either to himself or to Lavery.

"All she needs is someone to keep an eye on her. You could give this job to any one of half a dozen cops."

"But I'm giving it to you."

A muscle twitched in Drew's jaw—the only sign that he heard the iron in Lavery's soft voice. Whether he wanted it or not, he had the assignment. He knew just how far he could push, and when it no longer made sense to keep pushing. Lifting one shoulder in a half shrug of acknowledgment, he leaned back in his chair.

"Tell me about her."

If Lavery was pleased by his acquiescence, he didn't show it by so much as a glance. He shrugged.

"Most of it is in the report. She's Davis's personal secretary. Has been for about three years. He apparently got careless and she found some things that made her suspicious. She went snooping and came up with a tidy fistful of information, which she brought to us. Enough to get us into court. Now all we have to do is keep her alive to testify."

He closed the folder and tossed it across the desk. Drew picked it up but didn't open it. He'd already committed most of it to memory while he was deciding that he didn't want the assignment.

"Great. I'm going to be baby-sitting Nancy Drew."

Lavery fixed him with a cool look. "Ms. Sloane took quite a chance in coming to us. You, of all people, know what Davis is."

Drew's fingers tightened over the file, bending the edge of it. Yes, he knew what Davis was. He was a crime boss, to use an old term. Known but unprovable. On the surface, he was a respected member of the Los Angeles business community, but most of his money came from the drugs he smuggled into the country. The DEA knew it, but they hadn't been able to prove it. And he didn't limit himself to drugs. Prostitution, money laundering, outright theft—there wasn't a profitable crime in the city that Lester Davis didn't have his fingers most profitably dipped in.

He wanted Davis taken down. What he didn't want was to be sidelined, out of the action, babysitting a witness—no matter how important that witness.

Lavery watched him in silence. They'd worked together a long time and he could read Drew's thoughts better than most, which wasn't saying much. Drew Hunter walked very much alone. He revealed little of what he was thinking or feeling. He was closed in, controlled, and one of the best cops Lavery had. He was also on the ragged edge of burnout, whether he realized it or not. Keeping an eye on Kate Sloane was important, and it was almost equally important to get Drew away from the center of action for a few weeks. Besides, there were other reasons he wanted Drew on this assignment.

"We've got a leak in the department, Hunter." He drew the words out slowly, tasting their bitterness before letting them sour the air. Drew's eyes met his and there was no surprise in their cool depths.

"There had to be, considering what happened to Martinez and me. Martinez hadn't even talked to his wife about what we were doing. The only people who knew about it were cops. When it went bad..." He let the words trail off, his voice simmering with quiet, deadly rage.

"Martinez was a good cop. So are you, Hunter. You can't afford to go head-hunting. I want you out of town for a while," he said bluntly. "And I need someone I can trust to keep an eye on the Sloane woman. No one but you and I and a contact officer are going to know where you are. I don't want you calling in unless it's an emergency."

"If I take her to a known safe house, it won't be that hard to find us," Drew commented, knowing Lavery must have thought of the obvious.

"True." Lavery opened a desk drawer, pulled out a set of keys and tossed them across the desk. Drew caught them automatically, raising one dark brow in question.

"There's a small town in northern California. A distant cousin of my wife's just died and left the house empty. The heirs are in no hurry to do anything with the place, and they were happy to have tenants. A married couple who would take care of the place for a few weeks while they sort things out."

"Married?" Drew's brows rose. "Did Ms. Sloane agree to that?"

"We haven't even told her that she's leaving town. So far, Davis doesn't know who our witness is. We want to keep it that way, so we've tried to minimize our contact with the woman. You'll explain the situation to her."

"Great," Drew said, his tone sour. "I introduce myself to the woman, explain that her life is now in danger because she's done her civic duty, tell her she's going to have to go into hiding if she wants to stay alive long enough to testify and, 'oh by the way, I'm now your husband.'"

"That's a succinct summation," Lavery agreed. An almost imperceptible lightening of his dark eyes revealed an uncharacteristic humor. "I think you're just the man for the job."

"Thanks," Drew said without gratitude. Clutching the folder, he stood, ignoring the pain in his left leg when he refused to favor it.

"Hunter?" Drew turned at the doorway, raising a brow in question. "Be careful."

"I always am." He stepped through the door into the hustle of the outer offices.

"DAMN." THE CURSE was soft, carrying more frustration than heat. Drew adjusted his leg to a more comfortable angle on the pillow, trying to find a position where the ache wasn't quite so sharp. The doctors had warned him to give his leg time to heal, that he had to have patience. He had endless patience when it came to his job, but that left little to spare for things like injuries that were frustratingly slow to heal.

It was late—well after midnight—and the apartment was quiet, with that special kind of stillness that goes with the very early morning hours. He savored the stillness in the same way that he savored the fresh ground coffee he was drinking. He was a man who liked being alone, who appreciated solitude and the freedom that went with it.

Which was one of the things he disliked about this assignment—living with someone was not conducive to solitude. Drew lifted the Sloane folder off the back of the sofa, but he didn't immediately open it. He ran his thumb over the name stamped on the beige surface. There was something else that bothered him, but he couldn't quite put a finger on what it was.

Reluctantly he opened the folder. Kate Sloane's photograph lay on top and his eyes met the picture's. She was a pretty woman. Delicate features that were saved from being chocolate-box pretty by a strong chin that spoke of stubbornness. It was a black-and-white photo, but he knew from the paperwork that her eyes were green. They were thickly lashed and almost too big for her small features. In the photo, her hair was pulled back and it was impossible to do more than guess at its length. The description said it was brown, so why was he so sure that sunlight would find red highlights in it?

She was a pretty woman, but no prettier than half a dozen other women he could name off the top of his head. Why, then, did he feel such a surge of hunger when he looked at her picture? What was it about her that brought out this gut-level response, that made his fingers tense with the urge to see if her hair was as soft as it looked in the photo?

There was something there, something he couldn't define. His thumb brushed over her mouth and he could almost feel the softness of her lips, the moist warmth of her breath. He bit off a curse and shut his eyes, willing his body to relax. He was acting like a sex-starved teenager, getting aroused just looking at a photograph of a woman. Only this wasn't some stapled-in-the-stomach model, and he was a long way from being a teenager.

The folder hit the coffee table with a splat, the sound loud in the quiet room. Drew reached for his coffee cup and forced his mind away from the disturbing photograph and the strange effect it had on him. Time enough to think about the assignment tomorrow when he had to meet the Sloane woman.

He leaned his head back on the couch, cradling the mug against his chest, letting its warmth seep through the fabric of his shirt. The sound of the rain made him feel cut off from the rest of the world. Alone. Lonely.

He frowned. Now where had that thought come from? Loneliness implied a need for company other than his own.

A glance at the blank surface of the manila folder and he muttered a curse before getting to his feet. Damn, he must be getting old. Thirty-six seemed a bit early for mid-life crisis, but something was sure as hell wrong with him. Maybe it was all the painkillers they'd pumped into him when he was in the hospital. He'd stopped taking them as soon as he was conscious enough to argue with the nurses, but maybe the effects were still lingering. There had to be some excuse for the odd mood that seemed to have taken hold of him lately. He was damned if he was going to attribute it to Kate Sloane's photograph.

Drew limped into the kitchen and rinsed his cup out before setting it to drain. He moved over to the window that sat in the middle of one wall. Habit kept him to the side of the glass. It had been a long time since he'd been comfortable standing directly in front of a window.

The street was quiet, but an occasional car passed by, tires swishing on the wet pavement. Watching them, he suddenly wanted to know where they were going and what the passengers' lives were like. Did they have homes and families to go to on this damp night?

Now where the hell had that come from? His dark brows hooked together. What did he care whether they had homes or families? Since when did he stare out a window and wonder anything at all about the people passing by?

Annoyed by the uncharacteristically whimsical turn of his thoughts, Drew spun away from the window. The move was too quick for his injured leg and pain lanced through his hip as his knee buckled. He grabbed for the edge of the table, spitting out a curse that would have made a sailor blush. That, too, was uncharacteristic. He rarely cussed, rarely lost his temper.

But then he seemed to be doing a great many things he usually didn't do, he thought. Starting with getting shot three months ago.

He was limping heavily as he made his way back into the living room. Maybe Lavery was right to send him off on this baby-sitting job. Maybe he did need a rest, time for his leg to finish healing, time for him to get himself back on balance.

He hesitated by the sofa for a moment and then reached down to pick up the folder. Carrying it into the bedroom, Drew set it on the nightstand while he got ready for bed. It caught his eye as he slid beneath the covers. His hand on the light switch, he hesitated.

Annoyed at the compulsion he felt, he flipped it open and stared at the photo inside. Even on paper there was so much life in those features. Perhaps that was what made her linger in his mind. Was she as vibrant in person as she was on paper, or had the camera simply caught her at an unusual angle?

He realized he was running one finger caressingly over the photograph and he jerked his hand away as if stung, snapping the folder shut. A second later he clicked off the light.

He lay back against the pillows, letting the cool comfort of the sheets draw the ache from his leg. He was tired. Bone tired. That's all it was. Tomorrow, when he met Kate Sloane, he'd see that she was a very ordinary young woman. These strange feelings would disappear and he'd wonder why he'd ever thought it was any more than a flattering camera angle that made her seem so appealing.

BUT THE WOMAN who slipped into his dreams owed nothing to the flattery of camera angles. She was warm and alive, and Drew found himself reaching out to her, wanting to warm himself against her. She turned to smile at him, holding out her hands, taking his fingers in hers. At her touch, peace flooded through him, filling a void inside that he hadn't even realized existed.

He stirred in his sleep, disturbed by the intensity of his emotions, but she smiled again, pulling him closer, wrapping him in gentle warmth, and he relaxed back against the bed, sliding deeper into sleep.

KATE SLOANE LEANED against the wall beside the window and looked out at the wet street below. A car went by, tires kicking up sprays of water. In the light of a street lamp, she could see that there were two people in it. And then it was gone, leaving her to wonder where they were going, who they were, whether they were a couple in love.

She sighed and let her forehead rest against the cold glass. She didn't often have trouble sleeping, but tonight she'd tossed and turned until the sheets were a tangled mess. It was after midnight when she finally gave up trying to force sleep and got out of bed. She'd sipped a cup of cocoa, read a boring magazine and still sleep eluded her.

Well, maybe that was to be expected. She'd quit her job last week and had no particular prospects of finding another. Money wasn't a problem, at least not for a few more months. But she found that not having to go to work left her with a lot of time for thinking. And it seemed that a lot of her thinking centered around wondering where her life was going.

She was twenty-five years old, and she had no job, no family and no one in her life but a few friends. She wasn't wrapped up in her career, such as it was. She liked being an executive secretary, but she suspected that there were any number of other jobs she would have liked just as much.

Once she'd found out what Lester Davis was up to and had taken the information to the police, she'd had no choice but to quit. She couldn't work for a man who was involved in the kinds of things Davis was. She'd felt not the slightest pang of regret about leaving her job. There'd even been a twinge of relief, as if now she might be forced to make some changes in her life.

The problem was, she didn't know how to go about making those changes. She wasn't even sure what they should be. She just knew that, at twenty-five, she was alone and there didn't seem to be any reason to think that would change.

Kate sighed. In a city of eight million people, you'd think she could have managed to stumble across one man who made her pulse beat faster, a man who wanted a home and a family and someone to share them with. But if he existed, he was keeping himself well hidden.

A flicker of light in the street below drew her attention from her melancholy thoughts. There was a black car parked across the street, almost directly in front of her window, and there was someone sitting in it. She wouldn't have been able to see them if they hadn't lit a cigarette. Match light flickered over their features for a moment and then disappeared as it was extinguished. The car was dark and still again.

Not quite sure why, Kate shivered and drew back from the window. She hadn't turned on the bedroom light, so whoever it was couldn't have seen her. Just as she wouldn't have seen them if they hadn't lit that match. Suddenly uneasy, she lowered the blinds and turned away from the window.

Cupping her hands around her elbows, she told herself not to be an idiot. There was nothing sinis-

ter about someone smoking a cigarette in a parked
car at two in the morning. Okay, so it was a little
odd, but that didn't make it ominous. There was no
reason for Lester Davis's small eyes to come to
mind, no reason for her to think that that car had
anything at all to do with her. If the police had
thought she was in danger, they'd have provided
her with some sort of protection.

But all the talk in the world wouldn't make it any
easier to fall asleep. And when she did finally drift
off, her sleep was filled with dreams in which she
was running from something terrible but could
never quite escape.

Chapter Two

"Feldercarp!" Kate muttered the word under her breath.

With two bags of groceries and a leaky umbrella already balanced precariously in her arms, she was trying to maneuver her key into the mailbox. At least the mailboxes were sheltered by the archway that led to the inner courtyard, so she didn't have to get any wetter than she already was.

She gave a pleased murmur as the key finally hit the narrow slot and turned. A moment's concentrated effort and she'd managed to clutch the handful of bills and circulars and pull them out of the box. After that, it was a simple matter to drop them in one of the bags. Not so simple was getting up the stairs with all her burdens.

"The logical thing to do would be to put everything down and make two trips," she muttered. Talking to herself was safe enough since only her eyes managed to top the grocery sacks.

"But logic has never been one of your strong suits." She hefted the bags a little higher and tightened her grip on the umbrella. There was only one flight of stairs. Surely she could make it that far, even if her arms did feel as if they were being stretched by the weight of the bags.

She started up the stairs, shivering as a chill damp breeze worked its way under her collar. Every winter she swore she was going to move to a new apartment, one where the stairs weren't exposed to the elements, leaving the tenants at the mercy of rain, wind and dark of night. Or was that mail carriers who faced those hazards?

Giving a mental shrug, Kate continued to trudge up the stairs. The rain, which had been hardly more than a light mist for the past hour, increased to a drizzle. Water immediately found its way under her collar. Shivering, she doubled her pace up the stairs. Whoever said it never rained in California had obviously never spent the winter months in L.A.

She gave a small sigh as her foot finally hit the smooth surface of the walkway that circled above the courtyard. Ducking beneath the overhang, she restrained the urge to stick her tongue out at the increasingly heavy rain.

There was another juggling act when she reached her apartment door and tried to fit the key in the lock. But then it slid into place, the lock clicked open and she was able to step out of the cold wet afternoon into the warmth of her living room.

Kate released her hold on the umbrella, letting it drop to the carpet as she carried the groceries into the kitchen. She set the sacks on the counter and then bent to pull off the short black boots she wore, sighing with pleasure as she wiggled her stocking-clad feet.

She hummed softly to herself as she began unloading the groceries, sorting them as she went. She'd bought a few things for the elderly woman who lived downstairs, but there was nothing that couldn't wait until the rain eased up, as the weather report claimed it was sure to do anytime.

Before she ventured out again, she wanted a cup of hot tea and a few minutes to rest her feet. Maybe she'd get the classifieds out and see if there were any job possibilities.

She slid open a drawer and pulled out a knife to cut the tops off the carrots. Then again, maybe she wouldn't do anything productive at all. There was a new science fiction novel lying on the coffee table. Maybe she'd curl up with a cup of tea and—

"Ms. Sloane."

Without her volition, the knife continued its motion through the crisp carrot tops, hitting the cutting board with a soft thunk that sounded loud in the sudden silence. Kate stared at the board, thinking that she must have imagined it. She couldn't have heard a man say her name. That would mean—

"Kate Sloane?"

—that there was someone in the apartment with her.

"Ms. Sloane?" The voice was starting to sound impatient, but all Kate registered was that it was there—that it meant there was a man in her apartment with her.

When she didn't turn, she heard him move closer. She felt him reach for her, half saw a shadow of movement to her left and behind her, then reacted with a primitive instinct to survive. Spinning around, she swung out with the knife, hardly conscious that she still held it.

"Holy—" He jerked back, sucking in his stomach as the blade skimmed uncomfortably close. Kate had a vague impression of dark hair and a neat gray suit, but those things registered only subliminally. Her only conscious thoughts were that he was much bigger than she was and that she had to get away from him.

She jabbed at him again with the knife, less interested in causing injury than she was in clearing a path to the door. This time, though, he was ready for her. His hand closed over her wrist, halting the thrust. When she didn't immediately drop the knife, his long fingers tightened with brutal strength and pain shot up her arm. Gasping, her fingers numb, the knife clattered to the floor.

"Wait."

Kate wasn't interested in waiting. A man didn't break into a woman's apartment just to have a cozy chat. For a split second, they stood frozen, the knife gleaming dully at their feet. She hadn't bothered to turn on the overhead light, and she could make out few details in the dim light. But she didn't need to know the color of his eyes to know that she had to get away from him.

He still held her wrist in that implacable grasp. He made a movement with his other hand, but she didn't wait to see what he intended to do. She swung at him with her free arm, knowing it was a foolish effort. He fended the blow off easily, but he didn't have time to block her kick. She was aiming for his groin, but he twisted in automatic male response to that threat, and her bare toes caught him solidly on the thigh.

The results were more than she'd hoped for. His hand dropped from her wrist, his breath hissing out on a pained groan. His left leg—the one she'd kicked—seemed to give way and he dropped to one knee. Kate didn't wait for more. Darting by him, she raced for the front door. If she could just get outside, out where people could see them. Surely he wouldn't dare follow her, wouldn't try to drag her back inside.

But he was too quick. She'd barely reached the living room when his hand closed around her upper arm, leaving bruises as he dragged her to a halt.

She turned, hands raised, her fingers crooked like claws, but he was ready for her this time.

His foot caught her behind the knees, and Kate gasped as she felt herself falling. But the fall was broken sooner than she'd expected as she felt the softness of the sofa come up under her. Before she had a chance to draw a breath, he was following her down, pinning her to the sofa with his body.

Feeling the contrast between the cushions beneath her and the unyielding length of male flesh and bone above, Kate froze, her mind going blank as pure panic washed over her.

He was going to rape her, and there wasn't a thing she could do to prevent it. He had her pinned down so solidly that every breath she drew pressed her breasts more firmly against his chest, every move she made only seemed to twist her closer to him.

Mindless with fear, she tried to arch upward, desperate to throw him off. She might as well have been trying to move a mountain. She tried to bring her hands up, but he caught them easily, holding her wrists in one hand as he drew her arms over her head and pinned them to the arm of the sofa, leaving her completely helpless. She drew breath to scream, even though she knew that there was no one to hear her. But he anticipated that, too, and his hand clamped across her mouth, leaving the scream to reverberate only in her mind.

Kate twisted frantically, but there was no escaping the lean body above her, no easing of the hold on her wrists. A buzzing in her ears warned her that she was about to black out and she forced herself to go still. Struggling was getting her nowhere. If she fainted, she'd be completely helpless and he'd be free to do as he pleased with her.

If she'd hoped that her sudden quiescence might catch him off guard and cause him to loosen his hold, she was disappointed. There was no give, either in the fingers clamped around her wrists or in the hard, masculine frame that crushed her into the soft cushions.

She stared up at him, her eyes wide and frightened. Maybe she could reason with him. At least, maybe she could, if he ever took his hand from her mouth.

"I'm not going to hurt you." His voice was low and slightly husky, the kind of voice that would have been reassuring under other circumstances. But when she could feel every inch of him pressed against her, it was a little hard to be reassured.

"I'm going to move my hand. If you try to scream, I'll knock you out." There was no threat in the words, only a matter-of-fact statement. He wasn't trying to scare her, he was simply telling her what would happen. And Kate believed him. Perhaps he read as much in her eyes.

He lifted his hand slowly, pale eyes watching her. Kate might have tried to scream, despite his warning, if she'd thought that there was any possibility of being heard.

"Please." The word came out in a breathless rush. She couldn't have said just what she was asking for. For him to let her go, that he not hurt her, that he vanish in a puff of smoke. Any of the above would do.

"I'm not going to hurt you. I just want to talk."

"People who want to talk usually don't break into my apartment to do it!" *No, no. That wasn't what she'd meant to say.* She wanted to soothe him, not antagonize him. "But that's all right," she added quickly. "I don't mind. Just let me go and we can talk all you want."

She thought she saw his mouth quirk at one corner with something that might have been amusement, but the expression came and went so quickly it was impossible to be sure.

"I'm a police officer, Ms. Sloane."

Kate stared at him, torn between relief and doubt. If he really *was* a police officer, then she had nothing to fear. But anyone could say they were with the police. Wouldn't a real officer have knocked on the door and identified himself? Why would he have broken into her apartment?

"I do have identification," he said, reading her thoughts.

"Oh, that's all right, then." Her voice was too cheerful, too bright. She sounded downright perky. But she wanted him to think she believed him. She wanted him to let her go. "If you're a policeman, then there's no problem. You can let me go now," she added hopefully.

She'd been told that she had a lousy poker face and it was apparently true. One lifted brow expressed his distrust of her suddenly cooperative attitude. There was no slackening of the hold on her wrists, no easing in the pressure of his weight on her body. Kate gasped, trying to shrink deeper into the cushions as his free hand slid between their bodies, the back of his hand pressed against her breasts. There was nothing in the least sexual in the gesture, but she could have done very well without the intimacy.

He pulled his hand out from between them and flipped open the wallet he'd taken from his coat pocket. The badge glinted in the dim light, looking very official and reassuring. Of course, it could still be a trick, she thought, but he hadn't offered her any harm so far. Aside from a few bruises, that was, and she couldn't entirely blame him for those. Considering she'd tried to stab the man, he'd been relatively restrained. And the police *had* said they'd be in touch.

The shackling hold of his fingers on her wrists eased. A moment later, he lifted his weight from her, and Kate was able to scramble into a sitting position. She scooted as far away from him as the sofa allowed. What she really wanted to do was run out the door, but she didn't need him to tell her that he wasn't going to allow that to happen.

She reached for the wallet and he gave it to her without argument. He even stretched out one arm and turned on a lamp so that she could see it better.

Kate stared at the badge, wishing it could speak and tell her something about the man who carried it. "It looks very official," she admitted cautiously.

"It is official."

"Badges can be faked."

"Cynical, aren't you?" But there was more approval than resentment in his voice.

"You're Andrew Hunter?" she asked, looking at the ID.

"Drew Hunter."

Kate lifted her eyes to his face and felt her breath catch in her throat. The eyes that had seemed pale in the dim light proved to be a vivid ice blue, the pupils ringed in dark gray. Penetrating and beautiful. The rest of his features were even, his chin a determined thrust. Medium brown hair was cut short in a plain style. He was handsome in an all-American way, but it was those brilliant eyes that made his face memorable. She blinked and forced her gaze away from his face.

"How do I know you're really a cop?" Beautiful eyes or not, he'd still broken into her apartment and scared the wits out of her.

"Would you like me to tell you what you were wearing when you came to the station? Or tell you exactly what you know about Lester Davis? Where you went to school? How many jobs you've held since graduation? The name of your favorite restaurant?"

Kate was flipping through his wallet as he spoke, feeling not even a twinge of guilt for her nosiness. God knows, he'd intruded on her privacy more than a little. Turnabout was fair play. There wasn't much there. A couple of credit cards, a card that listed his blood type and that he was allergic to penicillin. Odd that it should seem necessary to carry that sort of information around with him. Unless he was expecting a medical emergency, one that might require a blood transfusion and antibiotics. She shivered and flipped to his driver's license.

The information it gave was succinct. Andrew Hunter. Age: thirty-six. Height: six feet, one inch. Hair: brown. Eyes: blue. That definitely did not do justice to his eyes. Blue did not even begin to describe them. She looked from the photograph to the man himself, studying his face and finding it no more revealing than the picture. Still, there was something there...

Making up her mind with characteristic abruptness, she tossed the wallet back to him. "Why didn't you just knock on the door?"

Drew slid his wallet back into his pocket and wondered why he didn't feel more relieved that she'd decided to accept him. Had he been hoping that her refusal to believe him would be the key to getting him out of this assignment?

"The building is being watched," he said, answering her question. "There was a chance they would recognize me. It wouldn't be in your best interest for them to know you had a cop as a guest."

"Uninvited guest," Kate pointed out crisply.

"Uninvited guest." Drew accepted the correction. "Invited or not, it wouldn't be wise for Davis to know you've spoken to the police about his activities."

"You think Mr. Davis is having me watched?"

"There's a car out front with two men in it. I don't think they're admiring the view."

"Is it a black four door with a dent in the front left fender?"

"It's gray and there's no dent." Drew looked at her, his eyes intent. "Have you noticed another car?"

"Sometimes. I thought I was being paranoid, seeing the same car everywhere." She shrugged. "I figured it was my imagination."

"No. I recognized one of the men in the car out front. He's worked for Davis for several years now. He's a small-time thug, not too bright, but very good at breaking arms and legs to order."

Kate shivered and drew her legs onto the sofa, wrapping her arms around her knees. Drew tried not to notice how small and vulnerable she looked. Nor did he want to see the fear that darkened her eyes to smoky green. Noticing things like that made it harder to think of her as a package he had to take care of until it could be safely delivered. They made her too human, too appealing. His job was to protect her. And he didn't have to be concerned with what she was feeling to do that.

"How would Mr. Davis find out that I'd talked to the police?"

"Lester Davis has connections everywhere, including the police department, unfortunately." The admission was bitter.

"So he knows what I saw, what I told the police?" Kate shivered again and her arms tightened around her knees as if she could hug the inner chill away.

"If he knew anything for certain, you'd be dead already." Kate recoiled as if the words had an actual, physical impact. Seeing the color drain from her cheeks, Drew regretted his bluntness. It had been too long since he'd dealt with the real world, a world where violence was shocking rather than just a part of life.

He felt a sudden, unwelcome urge to reach out and touch her, to reassure her, to tell her that everything was going to be all right.

Damn Lavery for giving him this assignment.

"Davis knows that there's been a leak, that we have new information," he continued. "You can't keep an investigation like this quiet. The fact that you quit your job is bound to make him look in your direction."

"But I couldn't continue to work for him," Kate protested, as if Drew had suggested she should have. "Not after I found out what he was doing."

Not with a face like that, Drew thought. Those eyes revealed every emotion, every thought. Davis would have known immediately that something was up. And she would have been dead hours later. Davis was nothing if not efficient.

"It still made you an obvious suspect," he said shrugging.

"So what are you doing here? I assume you're here to make sure I stay alive long enough to testify." Her eyes were steady on his, making it clear that she understood exactly what her value was to the police. And she was right. He was here to keep her alive so her testimony could nail Lester Davis. So why did he feel guilty that he was only here because she was valuable to the case?

"That's exactly why I'm here," he said, without **trying to soften the** agreement.

There was a brief pause while Kate digested what he'd told her so far. Drew felt a reluctant twinge of admiration. He had to give her credit for keeping a cool head. No tears, no protests that she should have been told about the danger inherent in agreeing to testify. Actually, if he remembered the report, she *had* been told and she'd agreed, anyway. *A cool lady,* he thought.

"So what happens now?" Kate asked, only the slight unsteadiness in her voice betraying any stress.

"Now we make sure you're safe." He wanted to approach the topic of moving her obliquely, selling her on it before he actually suggested it.

"You want to move me to a safe house?" she asked.

Drew's eyes jerked to her face in surprise. The last thing he'd expected was for her to anticipate all his careful arguments.

"Yes, we do," he admitted, half-resentful that she'd skipped a few of his planned steps.

"I've seen this plot on television," she said. "The police always move the witness to a safe house. And the witness usually ends up killed because there's always a bad cop who reveals the location of the house. Which always made me wonder why they call them *safe* houses," she finished thoughtfully.

"Life is a little different from television."

"But you already said that Mr. Davis has connections in the police department," she pointed out. "So what's to stop him from using those connections to find out where I am?"

She was quick, he had to give her that. It shouldn't have surprised him. She'd been quick to recognize what she'd stumbled on to in Davis's office and quick to act on it. And she'd been quick to react when she'd thought he meant her harm. Too quick for comfort, he admitted, remembering the gleam of the knife in her hand.

"The place we have in mind isn't an official safe house. And only myself and Lieutenant Lavery would know where you were."

Kate took a moment to digest that. Then, "What if I refuse to go?"

"Then we'll do our best to protect you here," Drew said grimly.

"You don't think I'd make it to the hearing, do you?"

"No."

He didn't add anything to the blunt denial. This was not the time to be softening his words. He wanted—had to have—her agreement. And if he could only get it by scaring her, then so be it. It wasn't as if he were telling her anything but the truth.

"So you break into my apartment, scare the wits out of me, physically attack me—"

"You were the one who did the attacking."

"—and then expect me to trust you enough to ride off into the sunset with you," she finished, ignoring his interruption. "How do I know you don't work for Mr. Davis? How do I know you're not a bad cop?"

"Because if I were, you'd already be dead."

And he could do it, Kate thought, looking into those ice blue eyes. If he had to, he could kill. He was right about who had attacked whom, though he could hardly blame her for reacting the way she had. When a man broke into a woman's apartment, she couldn't be blamed for not stopping to ask if he was with the police.

She looked away from him, rubbing her fingers absently over one bruised wrist. On the other hand, he hadn't hurt her, at least not deliberately. And what he was saying made sense. Hadn't there been a part of her that had known from the beginning that her life was never going to be the same once she went to the police with what she knew?

"Is this legal? Taking me to an 'unofficial' safe house, I mean? With just the two of you knowing where I am?"

"There's nothing illegal about it," Drew said carefully.

"But it's not officially sanctioned?"

"If it were, there'd be a lot more people who'd know where you were. The idea behind doing it this way is that no one would know. Is there anyone who'd worry if you weren't around for a few weeks?"

Kate didn't answer immediately, not because she didn't know the answer, but because she was suddenly reluctant to tell him what she suspected he already knew. If she'd been investigated as thoroughly as he said, then he had to know that there was no one who'd worry about her, hardly anyone who'd even notice her absence.

"No. No one would worry," she said at last, resenting him for making her say it.

"Good. That makes things easier."

Kate wasn't sure she'd have phrased it quite that way. Lonelier maybe, but rarely easier. But from his point of view it did make things simpler. She didn't have to be a cop to know that the fewer explanations that had to be made, the less chance of Lester Davis finding out what was going on.

Kate stood, suddenly restless beneath that cool blue gaze. She was aware of Drew Hunter's eyes following her, but she ignored him, at least for the moment. Picking up a soft pillow, she hugged it to her chest, feeling cold inside.

It had taken her three years to turn this apartment into a home, the first real home she'd ever had. The first place she'd lived for more than a few months. And now this stranger had burst into her life and was telling her that she was going to have to leave it and go with him to God knows where for an unspecified length of time, that she was going to have to leave behind everything she'd worked so hard to create.

"I wish I'd never seen those damn files," she said quietly.

Drew said nothing. He didn't need to. They both knew she was agreeing to go with him. She really had no choice.

RELUCTANTLY DREW ALLOWED Kate to take the groceries she'd bought for Mrs. Burnet down to her. Not that she seemed to think there was any question about her going.

"She's expecting me," she said, when he questioned the wisdom of her leaving the apartment.

"I'd rather you stayed inside."

"I can hardly ask an eighty-five-year-old woman to come out in the rain and climb an exposed flight of stairs and then carry a sack of groceries back down to her apartment," she said, as if pointing out the obvious.

"I don't like you going out."

"You can watch me the whole way." She sounded as if she was offering a consolation prize, Drew thought, gritting his teeth.

"What if Davis's men see you?"

"They've seen me any number of times today." Kate finished pulling on her boots and straightened, forcing herself to shrug as if the idea that hired killers might be watching her every move didn't chill her to the core.

"I don't like it."

"Mrs. Burnet needs her groceries. Her son usually looks after her but he's out of town this week and I said I'd keep an eye on her. I'll only be a few minutes."

And that seemed to be that, he thought, knowing he'd lost the argument.

Since the whole idea was to keep his presence hidden he didn't come with her, but Kate was vividly aware of him watching her as she crossed the courtyard. The feeling was at once reassuring and disconcerting—certainly it was nice to know that she had protection, but she wasn't accustomed to having her every move watched, especially not when the watcher happened to be one of the most attractive men she'd ever seen.

Not that that was relevant, she told herself as she tapped on Mrs. Burnet's door. It didn't matter to her whether Drew Hunter looked like Frankenstein's monster or Mel Gibson. The fact that he was much closer to the latter than the former was of no interest to her. None at all.

FROM HIS POSITION beside the window, Drew watched as Kate stepped into the apartment across the courtyard. He should have told her not to go out of sight, he thought. But then she couldn't really have thrust the sack of groceries into the spindly arms of the old woman who'd opened the door, and then dashed away. The idea was *not* to arouse suspicion.

When the door closed behind her, he turned and glanced restlessly around the apartment. He'd had plenty of time to study the layout while he'd been waiting for her to come home this afternoon. Time to fall asleep, too, he admitted, angry with himself for that lapse. He'd sat on the sofa to await her arrival, and the next thing he was aware of was the sound of her umbrella hitting the floor.

He still couldn't believe that he'd slept through her opening the door, or that he'd been thrown off balance enough that it had taken him several minutes to make his presence known. Things like that could get a man killed. Damned near *had* gotten him killed, he thought, remembering the gleam of light on the knife as it had slashed toward him. Wouldn't that have been a laugh, to survive all these years only to end up killed by a witness he was supposed to be protecting?

Kate came out of the old woman's apartment, saying something before she closed the door behind her. Her smile lingered for a moment, and Drew felt that same odd little jolt of recognition that he'd felt when he saw her photograph, as if he'd known her somewhere before.

She glanced up at the window, her smile fading, though he knew she couldn't possibly see him. Apparently just the thought of him was enough to ruin her mood. Not that he could blame her, Drew thought, wondering why it mattered. She'd done what was right; she had come to the police with what she'd learned, and as a reward her life was in danger. But at least she had a life, he thought bleakly. Martinez hadn't been given that option.

He stepped back from the window as Kate opened the door, watching her, trying not to notice how the damp, misty air had darkened her hair, making it curl around her face. The last thing he wanted was to notice how attractive this "assignment" was.

"I told her I'd be going on vacation for a few weeks, just driving around the country." Kate pushed the door shut behind her and reached up to run her fingers through her hair, shaking the water droplets from it.

"Good." Drew curled his fingers into his palms against the urge to feel the dampness of her hair for himself.

Kate's eyes met his for a moment, and he read uncertainty and a touch of fear. He restrained the urge to reassure her. She was better off—they were both better off—if she remained just a little bit frightened. Fear could make a person more careful.

"I guess I'll finish putting the groceries away," she said, breaking eye contact. Drew said nothing, letting her walk by him while he struggled with the absurd urge to put his arms around her and hold her until the fear went away.

It had to be lack of sleep, he told himself. He hadn't been sleeping well since the shooting. Nightmares woke him more nights than not. It must be catching up with him.

Marginally satisfied with that explanation, he turned and followed his reluctant hostess into the kitchen, stopping in the doorway when he saw her bending to pick up the knife he'd forced her to drop earlier. She straightened but didn't look at him. She set the knife on the counter and then brought the fingers of her left hand up to rub the bruises that were beginning to show on her right wrist. Bruises he'd put there, Drew thought, surprised that the realization disturbed him.

"Let me see."

Kate glanced up, her eyes startled as he eliminated the few feet between them and took her hand in his. She would have drawn back, but she was suddenly aware of a strange current that seemed to flow from where his hand held hers. Her gaze lifted to his face, but if he felt it, too, she couldn't read it in his expression.

Drew looped his fingers around her wrist, laying them over the faint blue bruises, bruises that would undoubtedly grow much darker by morning. Seeing the mark of his fingers on her pale skin, he felt a wave of self-anger that made no sense. She'd been trying to kill him, for God's sake. He could have hurt her a lot worse than he had and still considered himself justified.

"I'm sorry," he said gruffly.

"It's okay. I'd get pretty hostile if someone came at me with a knife." Kate managed a smile and told herself that she didn't really like the feel of his hand on hers. "I suspect you could have done a lot more damage than you did."

"Yes." Drew looked at her, his eyes as flat as his answer. She repressed a shiver and forced another smile. "I hope I didn't do too much damage when I kicked you. I noticed you were limping a minute ago."

"An old injury." Drew dropped her wrist and moved back a step, careful to balance his weight evenly on both legs, resenting that she'd noticed the slight limp.

"Well, it obviously didn't do it much good to have me kick you. I'm sorry."

"Forget it." The cool response and the fact that he didn't bother to look at her gave Kate a sudden urge to kick him again, harder this time. "It doesn't bother me."

"Good," she said brightly. "Then why don't you fix dinner while I start packing."

"Dinner?" Drew looked at her blankly, caught off balance by the sudden shift of topic.

"You know, the meal that most people eat in the evening. There's no sense in you sitting around like a bump on a log. The taxpayers are paying your salary. I'm a taxpayer and I don't see why I shouldn't get my money's worth out of you."

"I'm a cop, not a short-order cook."

"I'm sure you can manage," Kate said, giving him a cheerful smile that made him want to shake her. "If you need help finding anything, let me know."

"One suitcase," he ordered, turning as she walked out of the kitchen.

She didn't bother to respond, but at least he had the satisfaction of having had the last word.

Chapter Three

Kate rolled over and stared up at the darkened ceiling. She didn't need to look at the clock to know that she should have been asleep hours ago. Drew wanted to leave as soon as the sun came up.

Drew. Funny, how easily his name came to her, as if she'd known him a long time, as if they'd been introduced at a party, rather than having met over the flash of a knife.

Was he sleeping? Probably. This must be just part of the routine for him. Was there someone lying awake somewhere wondering if he was safe? A wife? Girlfriend? Somehow the image wouldn't come into focus. There was something about Drew Hunter that made her think of the Rudyard Kipling poem about the cat who walked alone.

She turned on her side and stared at the curtained window, wondering if the dark sedan was still out there. Her fingers plucked restlessly at the quilt that covered her. How was she supposed to sleep when her entire life had been turned upside down? Tomorrow she was to leave this apartment—her home—and go off with a man she didn't know to a place she didn't know, to wait for an unknown length of time before coming back to testify against the man she'd worked for. And after that, maybe a trial. And after that? Kate's mind shied away from thinking that far into the future. The near future was unnerving enough all on its own.

Was she a fool to trust Drew Hunter? What if it was all lies, all part of some plot to prevent her from testifying? But then, if that were the case, he could have killed her here and been done with it. She didn't doubt that Lester Davis was ruthless enough to do just that if he thought it necessary. She'd learned that much about the man during the three years she'd worked for him. Even if she—

Kate sat up abruptly, her train of thought scattered as she heard a sound from the living room. She sat there, her heart pounding, her ears straining for a repeat of the sound that had startled her. A low cry, perhaps a word too mumbled to understand. Drew? It didn't seem possible that he could sound so vulnerable.

But when the sound came again, she swung her feet out of bed and went to the door. Opening it just wide enough to slip through, she tiptoed into the living room. He'd fallen asleep with the light on, probably while reading, she thought, noting the book that lay on the floor next to the sofa.

The quilt she'd given him for cover was twisted around his hips, baring a somewhat daunting expanse of muscled chest dusted with jet black hair. One hand was flung over his head, the fingers trailing on the table at the end of the sofa. The other hand was twisted in the sheet beneath him, knotting the fabric as if clinging to a lifeline.

As she watched, he jerked in his sleep, the movement so abrupt that Kate jumped. His head twisted, his features going tight, as if he were in pain. He muttered under his breath and then cried out again. This time she thought she distinguished the word "no" but she couldn't be sure.

Obviously he was having a nightmare. She hovered uncertainly, curling her bare toes into the carpet as she debated whether or not to wake him. Certainly he wouldn't thank her for seeing him with his guard down. On the other hand, she couldn't just go off and leave him in such obvious distress.

She edged toward him, coming to a stop beside the sofa. She hesitated, not sure what to do next. Was there some special way to wake someone in the midst of a nightmare? Kate nibbled on her bottom lip, wishing she weren't so vividly aware of the way the lamplight gleamed on the muscles in his shoulders and the way his hair fell in a thick black wave onto his forehead.

He shifted and the quilt slid down another half an inch. She caught her breath, her eyes followed the line of silky black hair that arrowed down his flat stomach and disappeared beneath the edge of the quilt. Surely he wasn't naked. Was he? Ashamed of the unwelcome tug of curiosity, she bent and set her hand on his shoulder, shaking lightly.

"Drew?"

He moved with blurring speed. One moment, she was standing over him, looking into his flushed face. The next, she was flattened on his chest, her hands trapped under her, her breath stolen from her.

Frozen, she stared into the pale blue eyes only inches from hers, eyes that looked more than capable of murder. One of his hands was flattened across her back, holding her to him. The other was cupped around her chin, the grip anything but tender. Something told her that, if he chose, he could break her neck in less than a heartbeat.

She held her breath, not moving, though every instinct screamed for her to struggle. Something more powerful held her still. Drew stared up at her, the murderous rage in his eyes gradually fading as he recognized her, sorting her out from whatever nightmare images had followed him into wakefulness.

"Kate."

It was the first time he'd used her name and Kate felt it shiver over her in a featherlight stroke. The fingers cupped around her chin gentled, their touch becoming almost a caress.

"You were having a nightmare," she whispered. She was vividly aware that her breasts were pressed intimately close to the hard planes of his chest.

"Yes." His voice was low and husky, roughened by sleep.

"I . . . was trying to wake you," she said after a moment.

"Thanks."

His eyes searched her face, an intensity in them that made her tinglingly aware of the lateness of the hour, her own state of dishabille, and the fact that, as far as she could tell, he wore nothing but a slipping quilt for cover.

She should pull away. And so she would. Just as soon as she was sure that he was fully awake. The odd shivery feeling that was working its way up her spine was because the room was cool. It had nothing to do with the fact that her palms were flattened against the muscled width of his chest, allowing her to feel his every heartbeat. And she hardly noticed the way the dark stubble along his jaw made his eyes seem even bluer. Her knees only felt weak because he'd startled her.

And she certainly hadn't wondered, even for an instant, what it would be like if he were to pull her onto the sofa with him, wrapping the quilt around the two of them and—

"I couldn't remember whether or not you were supposed to wake someone who was having a nightmare," she said, bursting into speech and hoping he'd attribute her breathlessness to the awkwardness of her position.

With an effort, she looked away from his face and pressed upward against the hand still flattened along her spine. Was there an almost imperceptible hesitation before he released her, or was her imagination working overtime?

"I thought I remembered reading somewhere that if you woke a person having a nightmare, you could damage their psyche, but then it seemed to me that it couldn't be all that good for a psyche to just let you continue a bad dream."

She eased away from Drew as she spoke, first sliding to her knees on the carpet and then standing. Smoothing her hands over the sides of her nightgown, Kate tried to ignore the small voice that wished she were wearing black silk and lace rather than plain white cotton. It was a ridiculous thought, brought on by the lateness of the hour and lack of sleep, she told herself briskly.

Drew Hunter probably wouldn't notice her if she were wearing a mesh bikini, which suited her just fine.

DREW WONDERED WHY it had never occurred to him that white cotton could be so sensual. There was nothing in the least provocative about Kate's sleeping attire, unless you considered long sleeves and a knee-length ruffle sexy. He never had before, but there was something about it... Maybe it was the very innocence of the garment that made him want to strip it away and find out what lay beneath its prim facade.

Not that he didn't already have a pretty good idea of exactly what it concealed. Between the struggle earlier in the afternoon and having her crushed to his chest moments ago, there wasn't much about Kate Sloane's shape that he didn't know. But it wasn't the same as sliding his hands over bare skin, as molding the softness of her breast with his palm.

Drew shut his eyes and curled the fingers of one hand into a fist. What the hell was wrong with him? First, he'd spent time mooning over her photograph, and now he was lying here wanting her so much that he was grateful that the heavy quilt was still draped over his lap. Otherwise, his thoroughly unprofessional thoughts might have become more than a little apparent.

"Are you all right?"

Drew opened his eyes and looked up at Kate's anxious expression. Her hair was tousled from contact with the pillow and it fell around her face in shining, light brown waves. It had felt like the finest silk against his chest.

"I'm fine." He had to clear his throat to get the words out. Even then, his voice remained husky.

"Do you want to talk about it?"

"About what?"

"About your nightmare. I read somewhere that it helps to talk about it."

"I don't think that would help."

"How do you know? Talking about it might help you understand it."

"I understand it just fine," he said shortly.

"Are you sure?" She frowned down at him, unconvinced. "I read somewhere that a person sometimes thinks a dream is about one thing when it's really about something else entirely."

"I know exactly what this was about," Drew snapped. He swung his legs off the side of the couch, hardly noticing Kate's indrawn breath and then relieved exhalation when she saw the striped pajama bottoms.

He thrust his fingers through his hair, feeling a nagging ache behind his eyes. He wished he hadn't quit smoking. He wished he'd never heard of Lester Davis and never met Kate Sloane. He wished she'd take her virginal white gown and her concern and get out of his sight.

And more than anything, he wished he could reach out and put his hands on her hips and draw her closer. He wanted to pull her down onto the sofa with him and see if he could lose himself in her.

"I'm really very easy to talk to," she said, her voice full of soft concern.

Looking up at her, Drew noticed that the cool air had had a predictable effect and that the dusky peaks of her nipples were pressed against the thin white cotton of her gown. The sight had an equally predictable effect on his body and he bit back a groan as he dragged more of the quilt across his lap.

"Why don't you go back to bed?"

"Are you sure—"

"I'm sure." He softened the quick answer with a half smile. "I'm fine."

She continued to hover there, her eyes all smoky green with concern, so close he could smell the clean tang of the soap she'd used earlier.

"Go to bed, Kate. Please." Perhaps she heard something in his voice or read something in his eyes. Whatever it was, the message seemed to finally get through to her. She flushed lightly.

"Good night, then."

"Good night."

Drew watched her disappear into the bedroom and heard the soft snick of the latch clicking home. Elbows braced on knees, he dropped his head into the cradle of his hands.

This assignment was going to be the death of him, he thought, not sure he was kidding. Where Davis had failed, Kate Sloane just might succeed. And she wasn't going to have to lift a finger to do it. All she had to do was stand around and wait for him to make a fool of himself.

What was it about her that got under his skin? He was no green kid to fall to pieces over a pair of pretty eyes. There was just something about her...

Shaking his head, he lay back against the pillows and pulled the heavy warmth of the quilt up to his shoulders, his fingers unconsciously tracing the textured surface. It was handmade. The second foster home he'd been in, the woman had made quilts. He'd stayed with them more than a year, and when he left, she'd given him a quilt—blue-and-white stars—and she'd cried when he left.

That quilt had been one of the few stable things in his life. He'd slept under it in each succeeding foster home until he was finally old enough to leave the system. He wasn't quite sure what had happened to it after that. There'd been times while he was putting himself through college when he'd slept in his car and the quilt had served as a cover. But somewhere in the years between then and now, it had disappeared.

He hadn't thought of that quilt in years. Not until Kate had spread this one over the sofa. The moment he'd crawled under it, felt the weight of it settle around him, it had brought back a flood of memories.

She could have bought it, of course, but she hadn't. He knew, as surely as if he'd seen her working on it, that Kate had set each stitch herself.

What had she been thinking of while she worked on it? Certainly not that it would one day be used to cover a slightly burned-out, more-than-a-little-battered cop.

Drew's mouth curved in a half smile, his eyes drifting shut. It was ridiculous, of course, but it seemed to him as if the weight of the hand-stitched cover was somehow more warming than any purchased blanket could have been.

"CAREFUL. IT'S A GUITAR, not an old board, you know." Kate frowned down at him from her perch on the block wall.

"Feels more like an anvil," Drew muttered. Nevertheless he handed the case up to her as gently as if it were a Stradivarius.

She set it on the wall next to her and reached down to take the first of two large tote bags from him. They joined the suitcase and an enormous purse on top of the wall.

Staring up at the array of items, including the witness he was supposed to be protecting, Drew tried to figure out how his strict orders for her to pack one suitcase had been bypassed. Certainly he'd protested when he'd seen everything she'd packed. He distinctly remembered telling her that one suitcase meant just that and nothing more.

"I'm not leaving my guitar behind," she said flatly.

He looked at the set of her jaw and nodded reluctantly. "Okay." He'd never been musically inclined himself, but he understood that people could become very attached to their chosen instruments. "The guitar I'll allow, but what about all the rest of this stuff."

"There's not that much," she protested.

"I've seen entire circus troupes move with less baggage," he said acidly, eyeing the pile of canvas totes at her feet.

"This is my purse," she said, lifting an object that was almost big enough to qualify as a duffel bag. "You're not going to tell me I can't take my purse, are you?"

"Okay. The purse can go." He drew the sentence out slowly, loath to give more ground.

"And you told me to pack one suitcase," she pointed out, looking mildly injured.

He nodded again, even more reluctantly. He hadn't realized they made Pullman suitcases as big as that, but it *was* a suitcase and he *had* said she could bring one suitcase.

"That doesn't explain those things." He gestured to the two brightly colored bags that remained.

"That's some of my quilting." She looked surprised that he should need it explained to him.

"You're not taking them." He'd make his stand here.

"Of course I am. They don't weigh all that much. Besides, we're not flying anywhere, so it isn't like there's a weight limit, is there?"

"The idea was to travel light," he snapped. "We're going into hiding. You don't normally take your every earthly possession into hiding with you."

"Why not?"

"Why not?" Drew jammed his fingers through his hair and tried to think of a way to explain why not.

"If I'm going to be stuck with you, God knows where, for God knows how long, I'm going to need something to do, aren't I?" She asked it in the tone of someone dealing with a slow-witted child. "My quilting will give me something to do."

He looked at the stubborn set of her mouth, but he also saw the vulnerability in her eyes. He'd seen the way she'd looked at everything in the apartment, as if she might be leaving forever and wanted to be sure to remember it. And he couldn't guarantee that she *would* be back.

"All right, dammit! Bring the stupid things. Bring the whole damned apartment, if you want to. What's a little furniture when you're running from killers? Maybe we can hide behind the sofa when the shooting starts."

"Thank you." Wisely, she chose to ignore his sarcasm. She gave him a sweet smile and went to get her jacket.

Which was how he'd ended up shoving two totes, a suitcase, a guitar and a fifty-pound purse up onto the block wall behind Kate's apartment building. Not to mention getting Kate herself up there.

"I feel like a kid running away from home," Kate said as Drew heaved himself up onto the wall and straddled it.

"The Incredible Hulk couldn't manage to run with all this stuff," Drew muttered.

"Don't sound so cranky," she admonished him cheerfully.

"Cranky?" Drew stared at her, trying to remember the last time someone had called him cranky. Not since he was an infant, surely.

"Obviously you're not a morning person."

"Morning person?" He was starting to sound like a parrot, he thought irritably. "Not particularly."

"I should warn you that I am."

"Thanks. I'll keep that in mind."

"I'll try not to be too cheerful," she told him soothingly.

"I'd appreciate that."

Despite himself, Drew felt a smile tug at one corner of his mouth. Never in his life would he have imagined himself perched on top of a wall at six-thirty in the morning, having a conversation about whether or not he was a morning person with the witness he was supposed to be protecting. And he'd thought this job had just about run out of surprises.

THEY MADE IT ALMOST to Malibu before Kate gave in to the urge to look over her shoulder. She tried to make the gesture casual, as if she just wanted to see the Pacific Coast Highway from a new direction. But she discovered there really is no casual way to crane your head around to stare out the rear window of a car.

Of course, there was nothing to see. No ominous black sedan lurking just behind their rear bumper. No cars with personalized plates that read Goons or I Killer. Nothing but a perfectly normal assortment of cars. Any one of which could be carrying someone who wanted her silenced.

She caught Drew's sideways glance and shrugged self-consciously. "I suppose if someone is following us, they're not likely to put a sign on their front bumper."

"No. But there's no one following us." He accelerated around a delivery truck.

"How do you know?"

"It's my job." He could have left it at that. With most people he *would* have left it at that. But most people didn't have soft hazel eyes that tried to look unconcerned and failed.

"No one saw me enter your building last night. And no one saw us leave this morning. They don't even know you're gone." Which was a miracle considering the way they'd been loaded down like pack mules, he thought, but he didn't say it.

"I hope you're right." But she glanced over her shoulder again before facing forward.

On their left, the Pacific Ocean spread endlessly to the horizon. To the right, the Santa Monica Mountains pressed down, their quest for the sea blocked by the thin black ribbon of highway. The rains were gone, leaving the sky a pale blue and the mountainsides washed in bright spring green.

Drew was relieved to find that Kate didn't feel it necessary to fill every second with conversation. They'd been barely a block away from her apartment building when she pulled some scraps of fabric out of the tote at her feet and began sewing. Her fingers had been shaking so badly that it was a miracle she could even get the needle into the fabric.

He'd been shocked by the urge to reach out and close his fingers over hers, to still their trembling, to comfort her. Instead, he'd curled his fingers more tightly around the steering wheel and kept his gaze focused out the windshield. Offering comfort wasn't part of his job description. He was only concerned with keeping her safe, not with keeping her happy. He was surprised that it was necessary to remind himself of that.

Still, despite a few snags, like the amount of luggage she'd brought and his own tendency toward unwanted softness when it came to her, he was starting to think these next few weeks might not be completely unbearable. She knew how to maintain a silence and she didn't insist on changing the radio station every five minutes. That boded well for the remainder of the trip, anyway.

"THERE'S A GAS STATION up ahead. We'll stop there." Kate looked up from her sewing and glanced at her companion.

Two whole sentences. And only an hour and a half since he'd last spoken. If he wasn't careful, he'd become downright chatty. "Good. I could use a chance to stretch my legs." She folded her quilt block and slipped it back into the tote bag as Drew flipped on the turn signal and guided the car toward the exit.

He didn't speak again until he'd pulled up next to the gas pumps. "Don't go too far," he cautioned her as she reached for the door handle.

"I thought you said they hadn't followed us." Kate turned to look at him, feeling her stomach go tight at the warning.

"Nothing's guaranteed," he told her, his ice blue gaze unemotional. "Don't go far."

He got out of the car. Kate hesitated before following him. *Nothing's guaranteed.* The flat words—neither promise nor threat—sent a chill up her spine. *Nothing's guaranteed.* Including her own survival? she hazarded.

Setting her jaw, she pushed the door open and stepped out onto the pavement. If someone wanted to kill her, cowering in the car wasn't going to offer much protection. If Drew hadn't thought it was safe, he wouldn't have stopped. She hadn't yet made up her mind as to whether or not she liked Drew Hunter, but she trusted him. Keeping her alive was his job and there was something about him that made her believe that he was very good at his job. She certainly hoped her faith wasn't misplaced, she thought with slightly grim humor.

After getting the key from the gas station attendant, Kate went around the side of the building to use the bathroom. The ladies' room was stark but clean and she lingered, splashing water onto her face in an attempt to wash away the torpid feeling that came from sitting in the car all morning.

Staring at her reflection in the mirror, she was suddenly struck by a feeling of total unreality. It didn't seem possible that she was actually on the run. Running for her life. No matter how she tried, she couldn't make it seem real. It just wasn't possible that her life had changed so completely.

No amount of pretending could change the reality of what had happened. If she hadn't seen those documents... If she hadn't gone to the police with what she'd learned... Shaking her head, Kate smoothed the hem of her moss green camp shirt over her jeans. There was no sense in thinking about what if. She *had* seen the documents and she *had* gone to the police. She had no one to blame for the situation she was in except her own conscience.

Pulling open the door, she stepped out into the sunshine, wishing it could do more to warm the chill that seemed to have settled inside her. But it was going to take more than a sunny day to melt that chill.

She turned toward the front of the building where Drew was probably waiting impatiently. It would be nice if the man were a little more open and friendly. They were apparently going to be spending quite a bit of time together. Was he planning on spending all of it in dead silence?

Kate had gone only a few steps when she heard the sound of laughter coming from the back of the station. There was a moment's silence and then a sharp yip, followed by another burst of laughter. Without hesitation, she turned and moved toward the sound.

She circled the Dumpster that sat at the corner of the building and stopped abruptly. There were four boys standing in a semicircle. In front of them was a large dog of indeterminate parentage. He was braced on three legs, the fourth hung at an awkward angle, obviously broken. From the prominence of the ribs that showed through his shaggy coat, it was obvious that a broken leg was only part of his problems.

Kate's heart immediately went out to the injured animal and tears welled up in her eyes. Rage burned them away when one of the boys reached out and poked the dog in the side with a stick, hard enough to draw a yelp from him. It was immediately followed by a low growl, but they had the animal backed against a fence, unable to run away and obviously too weak to fight.

Kate was upon them before she was even aware of moving.

"What do you think you're doing?" she demanded, pushing her way between two of them and snatching the stick away from the youth who held it. She stopped in front of the dog and spun to face them, her eyes flashing angrily. "You ought to be ashamed of yourselves."

Surprise held them silent for a moment. A couple of them glanced over their shoulders as if assuming that she had reinforcements on the way. Seeing nothing but the blank wall of the garage, they turned back to look at the woman who stood like an avenging angel between them and their victim.

They were older than she'd thought and, for the first time, she registered that they were wearing gang colors. Kate swallowed but she didn't allow her eyes to flicker from theirs for even a moment.

"What did you think you were doing?" she demanded, deciding that maintaining the offensive was the best strategy.

"Who wants to know?" It was a tall, fair-haired boy who asked, the sort of boy who should be in a

Norman Rockwell painting, not standing on the cracked asphalt behind a gas station, tormenting injured animals.

"It looked as if you were tormenting this dog."

"And what if we were?" one of the others asked, sneering.

"I won't let you do it anymore." She wished the words would have come out more forcefully, but it was becoming obvious that the dog might not be the only one in need of rescuing. She tightened her hold on the stick and tried to look completely calm and confident.

"What if we said it was our dog?"

"I still won't let you torment him."

"You gonna stop us?" the blonde demanded incredulously.

"If I have to." Kate lifted her chin, hoping the sweat breaking out on her forehead would be attributed to the warmth of the sun and not to the cold fear creeping through her.

DREW CAME AROUND the side of the building in search of his missing witness and stopped abruptly. It took only an instant to interpret the scene before him. The young toughs, the injured dog and Kate standing between them, a stick clutched in her hands as if it was the only oar in a sinking rowboat. She looked like an avenging angel, but the stick was hardly an adequate weapon, angel or no.

One of the youths started toward Kate. Their attention was focused so completely on her that none of them noticed that there was a new player in the game. The tall blond kid reached for Kate. She edged back until she stood next to the dog, who growled warningly, whether at Kate or the boys facing them was anyone's guess.

In the few seconds it took him to reach the group, Drew debated his options. He could try to reason with the boys, try to make them see the error of their ways. Or he could simply give them a graphic demonstration of just how in error they were. The decision was really quite simple.

There was a startled cry from the two boys who had the misfortune to be first in Drew's path. He wrapped his fingers around the back of each neck and rapped their heads together with an audible thud. They staggered back and fell to their knees, clutching their hands over their skulls as if trying to hold them together.

The other two spun to face him, their eyes widening when they saw their companions' quick and painful fate.

"Hey, man!" The startled protest came from the blonde.

"Back off," Drew told him, his eyes like chips of ice.

"This ain't none of your business," the boy protested, looking both nervous and angry.

"She's my business." Drew jerked his head toward Kate. "Now back off."

The boy looked from his companion who remained standing to the two who were attempting to stagger to their feet. From there, he looked at the cold threat in Drew's eyes.

"We don't want no trouble, man," he mumbled sullenly.

"Wise choice."

Drew watched as they gathered up their dazed companions and disappeared through a break in the wooden fence that separated the gas station from the next lot. Satisfied that they were gone, he turned back to Kate. The blistering words he'd intended to utter died unspoken.

She'd tossed the stick aside and dropped to her knees next to the dog, reaching toward him.

"Don't!" Drew snapped out the command and took a quick step toward her, knowing there was no way he could pull her back before the dog reacted as any injured animal would and probably tear her throat out.

Before Drew could get to her, she'd put her hand on the dog's shaggy head, stroking gently and murmuring to him. The animal trembled, but to Drew's surprise he didn't so much as bare his teeth in her direction.

"They were tormenting him," she said. "He's hurt and they were tormenting him." She looked up at him, her eyes swimming with tears, hurt and anger tangled in her expression. "I'm glad you bashed their heads together," she said fiercely. "I wish you'd bashed the other two."

Drew opened his mouth, intending to make some comment about the stupidity of her actions, about how badly she could have been hurt, about fools rushing in and the fact that the dog was no concern of theirs. He looked from her to the dog, who looked as if it took every bit of strength he had just to remain upright on three good legs. He sighed.

"I wish I had, too."

"We need to take him to a vet," Kate said, stroking her hand gently over the dog's back.

He could have pointed out that they were, more or less, on the run; that if, by chance, someone managed to pick up their trail, lingering in this tiny town was hardly the smartest thing they could do. He could have made some comment about not drawing attention to themselves, or the need to keep moving. But he didn't say any of those things. Instead, he sighed again and pulled the car keys out of his pocket.

"I'll wait with him in case our friends come back. You go bring the car around and we'll try to coax him into the back of it. Maybe the guy out front knows where there's a vet."

He was rewarded by Kate's brilliant smile as she stood up and took the keys from him. She bent to pat the dog reassuringly.

"You'll be fine with Drew," she told him reassuringly. "He'll take good care of you."

Throwing another smile in Drew's direction, she sprinted off toward the front of the station. Drew watched her out of sight and then turned to look at the dog, who eyed him suspiciously.

"Why do I have the feeling that this is *not* going to be an isolated incident?"

Chapter Four

"We'll stop here for tonight."

At Drew's announcement, Kate blinked the tired fog from her eyes and sat up straighter. She glanced at the clock on the dashboard and saw that it was only seven. It felt much later. After almost no sleep the night before and their early start this morning, it seemed as if it should be past midnight.

Flipping on the right turn signal, Drew guided the car off the highway and onto a gravel parking lot. There was a quivery neon sign beside the road that announced the name of the motel. Kozy Korner, it said in mottled pink letters. If she hadn't been too tired to care about anything but a hot shower and a bed, the cute spelling would have made Kate flinch.

"I was beginning to think you were going to drive all night," she commented as Drew shut the engine off.

"I'd planned on being a lot farther along by now," Drew said. "If we hadn't been delayed..."

"By 'delay,' I assume you're talking about the time it took to see the dog settled."

"It *did* cost us a good portion of the afternoon," he pointed out.

"You could no more have left him there than I could have. You were just as relieved as I was when the vet said he could patch him up. And I saw the money you gave him to pay for his care until he could find a home for him."

"I didn't say I wasn't glad the dog was going to recover." Drew heard the edge that temper gave his voice and stopped to draw a slow breath. "All I said was that we lost a lot of time," he finished in a carefully controlled tone.

"It was worth it," Kate said firmly.

Drew lifted one shoulder in a half shrug, unable to argue and unwilling to agree. "I'll go check us in. You wait here. The fewer people who see you, the better," he added, forestalling any possible argument about his autocratic order.

The reminder of just why the two of them were here, at this dumpy little motel, on an obscure highway in the middle of California, sent a chill through Kate. She'd almost managed to put Lester Davis and the possibility that he wanted her dead out of her mind entirely.

"I thought you were sure they hadn't followed us."

"They didn't follow us this morning, but by now they've probably figured out that you ditched them. The chances of them getting this far are slim. But the less visible you are, the safer you'll be. You haven't exactly been invisible so far."

"I suppose you're talking about the dog again," Kate said. Even in the marginal light that illuminated the car's interior, Drew could see the way her chin firmed.

"Well, it's a sure bet that the owner of that gas station would remember you. And the vet. Not to mention those four young punks you tangled with. If anyone was looking for you and they got that far, they'd know they were following the right woman. They'd know you weren't traveling alone. And they'd know what kind of car we're driving." He sighed tiredly and thrust his fingers through his hair. "And the way my luck has been lately, one of those people had a photographic memory and they'd remember the license plate number."

Hearing him lay the facts out like that made Kate swallow hard, but her chin didn't come down even a fraction of an inch. "I'm sorry if it's going to cause trouble, but I'd do it again. The dog was hurt. I couldn't just walk away from him."

Drew's eyes skimmed her face, unreadable in the dim light. "No, I don't suppose you could have."

And she supposed she could interpret that any way she pleased, Kate thought as he pushed open the car door and got out. She watched him until he reached the door marked Office and pulled it open.

Leaning her head back against the seat, she closed her eyes, letting exhaustion wash over her. Forty-eight hours ago, she'd had nothing more pressing to worry about than finding a job before her savings ran out. Now she was wondering whether she was going to live long enough to see that.

No, that wasn't entirely true. She opened her eyes and frowned at the architecturally uninspired building in front of her. Despite everything, she wasn't as worried about her survival as she might have been—as she should have been. Something about Drew Hunter made her feel safe. He'd keep her alive, at the cost of his own life, if it came to that.

She shuddered, feeling a chill that went all the way to her bones. God, what a mess she'd gotten herself into when she stumbled across those files. For a moment, she wished that she was the sort of person who could have turned a comfortably blind eye to her employer's illicit activities. It had been a decent job. Lester Davis had been tolerable to work for. If she hadn't been so damned efficient, she wouldn't have found those files and she could have continued with her life, blissfully ignorant.

She was so absorbed in her thoughts that she didn't notice Drew leaving the office and walking to the car. She jumped when the door beside her was suddenly pulled open. Her head jerked around so quickly that she actually felt dizzy for a moment.

"Don't do that!" she snapped, her voice sharp with the quick rush of adrenaline.

"Sorry. I assumed you'd seen me." Tiredness put an edge to Drew's husky tone as he stepped back from the open door.

"No. I'm sorry for snapping." Kate passed her hand over her face, her fingers shaky with fatigue and nerves. "I'm a little uptight," she said, offering a thin smile by way of apology.

"You've got reason." Drew opened the back door and reached for his duffel bag. "Which bag do you want?"

Kate gestured to one of the totes, too tired to even make a token offer to carry it. She swung her legs out of the car and stood, arching her back to ease the stiffness of too many hours in the same position. Wearily she followed Drew, watching as he set down her tote bag and slid the key into the lock. He pushed the door open with his shoulder, reaching in to flip on the light before stepping into the room.

She saw him give the room a quick, searching glance before turning to gesture her inside. She could have pointed out that the likelihood of finding someone lurking in a room at the Kozy Korner Motel seemed slim, but she knew his caution was more habit than expectation. What must it feel like to have to check out every room you entered for potential danger? she wondered. And then it occurred to her that she was going to learn exactly what it was like.

She heard Drew set her tote bag down and turned to thank him, her hand already going out for the room key. The polite good-night died unspoken as she saw him shut the door—with him on the inside. Her eyes swiveled from his lean figure to the twin beds set neatly against the wall and then back to him.

"You only got one room?"

"Just one." His eyes were ice blue and ready for an argument.

"Do I get any say in the matter?"

"No." There was no attempt to soften the blunt answer. "Protecting you is my job and you're not getting out of my sight until Davis goes to trial."

Kate closed her eyes for a moment, feeling incredibly tired. She opened them again and looked at him, reading the determination in his gaze and knowing that she could protest till she was blue in the face and she wouldn't get anywhere. With a sigh, she reached up and pulled the elastic band from the ponytail that had held her hair since before sunrise. Running the fingers of one hand through her loosened hair, she bent to pick up the brightly colored tote. Straightening, she looked at her companion.

"Do you want to check and see if there are any assassins lurking in the bathroom before I take a shower?" She gained some satisfaction from the quick look of surprise that flared in his eyes at her easy acceptance of the situation.

"I think the bathroom should be safe enough," he said slowly, watching her as if waiting for the objection he knew had to be coming.

Kate took considerable pleasure in giving him nothing more than a pleasant smile before disappearing into the bathroom and closing the door.

THOUGH SHE WOULD HAVE liked to stand under the shower for at least twenty-four hours, Kate forced herself to remember that she wasn't the only one who'd spent the day traveling and limited herself to only ten minutes. She toweled herself dry and pulled on a fresh pair of jeans and a loose T-shirt, but left her hair to fall in damp waves on her shoulders.

"Shower's all yours," she announced cheerfully as she stepped into the room. Drew turned from the bed where he'd tossed his duffel and nodded.

"Thanks." And a moment later, the bathroom door shut behind him.

"Well, at least I don't have to worry about him talking my ear off," Kate muttered under her breath. "A chatterbox, he ain't."

Shrugging off Drew's taciturn behavior, she tossed her tote bag on the other bed and began rummaging through it. She pulled out a small brass alarm clock and set it on the night table. The clock had been one of the first things she'd bought for herself when she got her own apartment and she hadn't wanted to leave it behind. Next came a small tan teddy bear, barely five inches high, wearing a red ribbon around his neck. He was settled carefully on the pillow.

She heard the shower go on and wondered if lots of nice, hot water would improve her companion's mood. She was sure there was a human under the impenetrable surface. She'd caught glimpses of him once or twice. Last night, certainly, when he'd had that nightmare. And the way he'd handled the injured dog today had shown a definite humanity. Despite his remarks about lost time, she'd seen the absolute patience he'd shown when he was coaxing the big animal to get into the car, as well as the anger in his eyes when he'd seen the animal's abused condition.

Yes, there was definitely a human inside Drew Hunter somewhere. It might take a little time to coax him out, but it didn't look as if she was going to have much else to do over the next couple of weeks.

A knock on the door interrupted both her unpacking and her thoughts. Going over to the door, she peered through the peephole. The boy standing on the other side of the panel could have posed for an advertisement for an average American teenager. From the shaggy layer of dark hair, to the T-shirt displaying a logo for a rock band whose name Kate didn't recognize, to the faded jeans, he could have been any kid from any high school anywhere in the country. The pizza box balanced on his hand made the reason for his presence immediately obvious. Which was why Kate didn't hesitate to open the door.

"You ordered a pizza?" The words hovered somewhere between statement and question.

"Probably." Drew must have remembered that they hadn't stopped for dinner, she thought. "Just set it down over there. What do I owe you?"

He named an amount and Kate turned to get her purse. "That your guitar?" he asked, his eyes lighting on the case propped up in the corner.

Kate turned to look at it, surprised. Obviously dinner wasn't the only thing Drew had thought of.

"Yes, it is. Do you play?"

"Yeah. Electric, mostly, but I got an old acoustic, too. You like Clapton?"

"Of course." Vaguely Kate was aware of the cessation of sound as the shower was turned off.

"You know 'Layla'? I'm learning that now."

"It's a great song."

"The greatest." His eyes shining with enthusiasm, he crooked his hands to hold an invisible guitar. His vocal rendition of the appropriate chords left something to be desired musically, but he made up for it with enthusiasm.

Biting her lip to hold back a smile, Kate wondered if he provided impromptu concerts with every pizza delivery, and just how she could politely cut this one short so that she could open the box to discover the source of the wonderful smells that were permeating the room.

As it happened, she didn't have to worry about cutting the concert short. Drew did that for her.

The moment he shut off the shower, he'd heard the pained sounds coming from the next room. Thinking that Kate was either desperately ill or under attack, he jerked a towel from the rack and wrapped it around his waist. Drawing his gun from the shoulder holster he'd hung over the hook on the back of the door, Drew yanked open the door, thinking to gain the element of surprise.

He definitely accomplished that.

Startled by the sound of the door banging back against the sink, Kate and the Clapton wannabe jerked their heads toward Drew, their eyes widening at the sight of him standing in the doorway, soaking wet and naked but for a towel and a .38.

The concert ended abruptly. A particularly complex vocal riff concluded on a high squeaky note that no guitar could ever have duplicated. The three of them stared at one another in stunned silence.

"You ordered a pizza," Kate said, after a moment when it seemed as if the room's other occupants had turned to marble.

"A pizza." He'd forgotten the damned pizza, Drew realized. Forgotten to tell Kate he'd ordered it; forgotten it was going to be delivered. The kid with Kate must be the delivery boy. Why was he holding his hands in such a strange position?

"I heard noises," he said, his tone accusing.

"I was just playin' a riff, man." The boy's voice broke, skidding into a falsetto.

"A riff?" Drew had lowered the gun as soon as he realized that Kate was in no danger. But the gesture didn't seem to offer much reassurance, judging by the glazed look in the kid's eyes.

"On the guitar," Kate explained when the boy seemed incapable of speaking. She bit her lip when Drew's brows rose, nearly meeting the wave of dripping wet hair that fell onto his forehead.

"Here." She held out a twenty-dollar bill to pay for the pizza, but there was no response from the delivery boy, unless you counted the bobbing of his Adam's apple. Kate finally stepped forward and pushed the bill into the hand that was still crooked around the neck of his air guitar.

He jerked as if her touch were electrically charged, his fingers closing convulsively over the bill. He didn't take his eyes from Drew as he started edging toward the door.

"I didn't mean to startle you," Drew offered. "I thought there was a problem."

"That's okay, man. No problem. Really. No problem." His mouth twitched toward a smile, but couldn't quite make it. He bobbed his head. "No problem." He groped behind him for the doorknob, unwilling to take his eyes from Drew's dripping figure.

"Keep the change," Kate said kindly, though she doubted that he heard her. She doubted he even remembered her existence.

"No problem," he said again as he got the door open.

"Nice talking to you," Kate offered, her voice choked.

"No problem." He pulled the door open, shot one last terrified glance in Drew's direction and then darted outside, slamming the door shut behind him. A few seconds later, they heard tires spinning on gravel and the grinding of gears as he completed his escape.

Kate promptly collapsed on one of the beds, her contained laughter spilling out. Drew glared at her, feeling like a fool and yet unable to see how he could have reacted any other way.

"Why did you answer the door?" he demanded angrily.

"Because he knocked." She didn't even have the decency to stop laughing long enough to answer him. Drew stepped back into the bathroom to pick up his holster and shove the gun into it.

"I suppose if Lester Davis had knocked, you would have opened the door?" he inquired.

"If he was carrying a pizza." She put her hand over her mouth, but it was not enough to stifle her giggles. "His face when you came out..." The sentence trailed off in renewed laughter.

"How the hell was I to know that wailing was supposed to be a guitar?" he snapped. "It sounded like someone was killing a cat."

That set her off on another fit of laughter. "His face when you came bursting out of the bathroom like the Lone Ranger... Only without the mask. Or much else."

"You shouldn't have answered the damned door," Drew said accusingly, trying not to notice the way her nose wrinkled when she laughed.

"Sorry." She didn't sound in the least sorry. "I guess I'm just not used to seeing assassins lurking behind every piece of pepperoni."

"You'd better get used to it."

"I'll try." Her humble look might have been more effective if she hadn't spoiled it by giggling again. "Maybe I'd better stick to plain cheese from now on. It'll give them less to hide behind."

Drew glared at her. The truth was, he was angry at himself more than at her. He should have remembered to tell her about ordering dinner. And if he'd forgotten that, he should at least have remembered it when he heard the kid doing his bad imitation of a guitar.

He rammed his fingers through his hair and glared at Kate again. The only effect it had was to make her giggle harder. Dammit all. Did she have to be so appealing?

Looking over her shoulder, he caught sight of his reflection in the mirror on the dresser. His hair stood up in dark waves, reminding him of a cartoon of an electrocution victim. Water beaded his bare torso. The white towel clung crookedly on his hips. And clutched in one hand was the shoulder holster, complete with gun.

He looked like an idiot. And he must have looked even more ridiculous bursting out of the bathroom like a madman, gun at the ready. No wonder that kid's eyes had bulged out so far they could have been scraped off with a stick.

"I suppose we can count on the delivery boy remembering us, if anyone comes looking," Kate said through her giggles. "Especially you. I think he'll remember you the rest of his life."

"He'll probably never play guitar again," Drew said, his mouth twisting in a reluctant smile.

"For a while there, I thought his fingers might be permanently frozen on an F chord. Which would severely limit his repertoire."

"Well, if he sounds as bad on a real guitar as he does on a fake one, I don't think the world has suffered a real blow."

The reluctant smile became a full-blown grin as he remembered the boy's stammering departure. "His voice may not drop until he's thirty," he said on a chuckle.

Kate felt her breath catch, her eyes widening at the way the smile transformed his features. She'd thought him handsome before, but when he smiled...

She swallowed hard and dragged her eyes away, suddenly wondering if she wouldn't have been safer staying in L.A. There were more kinds of danger than the overt one offered by Lester Davis. And she had the distinct feeling that Drew Hunter was a prime example of one of them.

THE LAUGHTER SERVED to ease some of the tension. It made them a little less strangers and a little more companions. They were a long way from being friends. Actually Kate couldn't quite imagine ever being friends with Drew Hunter, but if they were going to be stuck with each other for an undetermined length of time, it would be nice to be on friendly terms, at least.

After they shared the pizza, Drew turned on the television to watch the news. Kate wasn't sure at what point the tension of the past couple of days and their early-morning start caught up with her. She was aware of the newscaster's voice droning on, but the words were starting to slur together. As soon as the news was over she'd go to bed. At least, she would once she figured out how to go about doing that while sharing a room with a man she'd known barely thirty-six hours. She'd have to give that some thought. Just as soon as the news ended. . . .

She wasn't aware of Drew getting up to switch off the television. Nor of him coming to stand beside her bed, his expression unreadable as he looked down at her. She stirred slightly when he bent to lift her up, tugging the covers down before easing her back against the pillows.

He hesitated a moment, frowning at the snug jeans. He finally reached down and loosened the button at the top, trying to ignore the silky feel of her skin against the backs of his fingers. He pulled the covers up over her, but didn't move away immediately.

He glanced at the clock, at the little teddy bear and then back down at the woman who'd set them in place. The motel room already felt like more of a home than his apartment did after he'd lived there for five years. He stared down at her, his pale eyes brooding, and wondered whether he wasn't in more danger now than he'd ever been in his life.

BY MORNING, HE'D BEEN able to put the odd sense of danger from him, chalking it up to proximity and too little sleep. Kate was his job, nothing more, nothing less.

They drove throughout the day, stopping only for lunch and to fill the gas tank. Kate questioned the route he was taking—zigzagging up the state, adding miles to their journey.

"It's harder to trace a circuitous route," he said. He looked at the speedometer and eased his foot off the gas. He didn't want an encounter with the highway patrol any more than he wanted one with Davis's men. "If anyone manages to follow us part way, it will be harder to figure out where we're going," he added.

He glanced across the car at her, feeling his jaw tighten when he saw the animation momentarily drain from her face, the way it did whenever she was reminded of the reason for the journey. It left her looking altogether too fragile for his peace of mind.

"Why did you come to us?" he asked abruptly.

"The police? Why did I go to the police?" The question seemed to surprise her.

"Most people would have looked the other way. A few would have demanded a piece of the action."

"I think they'd have ended up wearing concrete shoes," she said slowly, looking out the window at the passing scenery. "I don't think Mr. Davis would have taken kindly to anyone making demands like that."

"No, he wouldn't. But that doesn't explain why you didn't just look the other way."

"I couldn't," she said, sounding almost surprised that he could ask. "What he's doing is wrong. If I ignored it, then I'd be just as guilty as he is."

"Or smart enough to look out for yourself," Drew commented dryly.

"That, too," she admitted with a smile. The smile faded almost immediately. "He'll kill me if he finds out that I'm your witness, won't he?"

"He's probably already figured it out by now. Your disappearance is as good as an admission of guilt." He paused, giving her the chance to point out that it hadn't been her idea to run. She met his look, saying nothing, and he realized that she must have known that from the start. His reluctant admiration for her went up another notch.

"As for killing you, that's why we're moving you to someplace he can't find you."

"What if he does find me? What if he sends someone to kill me?"

"Then I'll just have to get them first." The words were spoken coolly, without a hint of doubt that he could do just that, without a moment's hesitation for what he might have to do to protect her.

Kate shivered. There was something frightening and yet oddly reassuring about Drew Hunter's ruthless determination. She was suddenly very glad they were on the same side. She wouldn't want to have him as an enemy.

Drew sensed her uneasiness, but kept his eyes resolutely on the road in front of him. It was his job to keep her alive so that she could testify, not to shield her from the realities of the situation.

SINCE HE WANTED to arrive at their destination early in the day so that he could take a look at the town, Drew had already decided that they'd be spending one more night on the road. They stopped at a motel on the edge of a small town less than a hundred miles from their destination.

This time there was no question about their sharing a room. In fact, it felt so natural that Kate might have worried about herself if she hadn't been too tired to worry about anything but hot water and a soft bed.

It was after ten when they stopped. Kate pulled her nightgown on after she showered. She stared at her reflection in the steam-fogged mirror. It was the same gown she'd worn two nights before when she'd awakened Drew from his nightmare. It was a perfectly modest nightgown, knee length, long sleeved, with a shallow scoop neck. It even had a ruffle at the hem. No one could possibly accuse it of any overt allure. So why was she hesitating about walking out of the bathroom?

She nibbled on her lower lip. Was it that she didn't know Drew? Or was it that she knew him too well? Not that she could say she knew him at all. She suspected there weren't very many people who did know him. But spending two days and nights together did tend to force a certain intimacy. She thought they were developing a sort of tentative companionship. He'd actually talked to her today.

Which should have made it easier to contemplate sharing a motel room with him, right? He wasn't quite as much of a stranger as he had been the night before.

Which was exactly why it was harder to open the door and walk out into the room. Kate sighed at the illogic of it and turned away from her reflection to open the door.

Drew had turned on the television and was watching a situation comedy that hadn't been particularly funny even before it went to reruns. He'd been trying not to think about how little distance lay between the room's two beds and was annoyed with himself for even noticing such a thing.

When he heard the bathroom door open, he looked up, relieved to have his thoughts interrupted.

The relief disappeared the moment he saw her. She was wearing that same damned virginal nightgown she'd worn two nights ago. White cotton with just a hint of lace at the neck, it exposed less flesh than the T-shirt she'd worn all day. There was nothing in the least alluring about it. So why did the sight of her in it make him feel a hot rush of arousal?

"The shower's all yours," she said, her voice a shade brighter than necessary.

"Thanks." Drew's jaw hardened in self-directed annoyance. He stood as she moved farther into the room. He caught a whiff of her scent, a mixture of soap and toothpaste. Nice, homey smells that had no business making him think of cool sheets and warm skin.

"Better get some sleep," he growled as he brushed by her. The bathroom door snapped shut with more force than was strictly necessary.

By the time he'd finished his shower, he'd managed to convince himself that he was overreacting. There was nothing wrong with noticing that Kate was an attractive woman. And that's all that was happening. He was just a normal man reacting to an attractive woman. And if the response seemed more gut level than that, then it was strictly his imagination.

Which didn't mean he wasn't just as glad to find that she was already asleep when he stepped into the room. If it occurred to him that pretending to be Kate's husband until the time came for her to testify was not going to be as easy as he'd anticipated, he put the thought from him as he slid between the covers.

Tomorrow they'd reach the town of Hayfield, where they were going to be staying. It would be easier to ignore her undeniable attraction then. They'd be sharing a roof but not a bedroom, and he refused to admit to even the slightest twinge of regret at that thought.

Reaching out to snap off the light, Drew let his eyes linger on the soft curve of Kate's cheek, the tangle of pale brown hair that spilled over the pristine white pillow. Why couldn't it have been a nice little old lady who'd brought in the evidence against Davis?

There was a click as the lamp flicked off. Drew sank back against the slightly lumpy pillow and closed his eyes. A good night's sleep was all he needed.

HE DIDN'T KNOW how long he'd slept when the nightmare began. Nor could he have said how long he lay tangled in it, watching events unfold, knowing what was going to happen, yet also a participant, unable to stop what was to come.

There was Martinez turning toward him, his teeth gleaming against his swarthy skin as he started to say something about how long it had taken Drew to get back with the coffee. And then his eyes widened in surprise as a neat round hole appeared in the middle of his forehead.

Drew felt the sting of hot coffee spilling over his hands, heard as if from a great distance the pop of gunshots as he reached for his weapon. And then he felt his leg go out from under him, felt the night-cooled sidewalk come up beneath him. There was no pain, though he knew he'd been shot. Martinez was dead. His partner was dead. Martinez was dead.

The words repeated themselves over and over again as he lay there, bleeding, waiting for whoever had fired the shots to come and finish the job, knowing he couldn't lift a finger to stop it from happening.

He woke abruptly, coming upright in the bed, his breathing fast and hard, his body damp with sweat. Martinez was dead. Though it had been months since the shooting, each time the nightmare came, it was as if it had just happened and the pain was still raw and new, churning in his gut.

It was over. There was nothing he could do. Just as there'd been nothing he could do at the time. As if it had been preordained that Martinez would die that night. And that he would survive. Only there hadn't been anything mystical about the shooting. It had been a hit, plain and simple. A hit that had been only half-successful. Because he'd survived. And he was going to continue to survive, if only for the sheer pleasure of bringing down the man responsible for his partner's murder.

"Sometimes it helps to talk about it." Kate's voice came out of the darkness, soft as a whisper.

Drew jerked toward her, his pulse too fast, dream-induced adrenaline still pumping through him.

"I thought you were asleep." There was a snap to the words that made them an accusation.

"I was, but you were muttering in your sleep."

"Sorry." In the darkness he could make out no more than the shape of her beneath the covers.

"Sometimes it helps to talk about it."

For a moment, he was caught by a shocking urge to do just that. He hadn't talked about the nightmares with anyone, not even the department shrink who'd carefully explained all the phases he was going to go through in dealing with the natural grief and guilt that came with being a survivor.

"There's nothing to talk about. Just a bad dream. Sorry I woke you." His tone was dismissing, but he couldn't quite bring himself to lie back down. He'd learned that if he went back to sleep too quickly, the dream sometimes returned.

"Who's Martinez? You said the name in your sleep."

"He was my partner. My friend," he added, almost under his breath.

"Was?" Kate was quick to pick up on the implications of that.

"Go back to sleep, Kate." Drew's voice was taut.

"Sometimes things aren't so bad if you talk about them." Her voice was husky with sleep, coming out of the darkness, running over his bare skin in the lightest of caresses.

"This isn't a nightmare full of boogeymen, Kate. It's a memory. And no amount of talking about it is going to make it better."

"What happened to Martinez?" she asked, as if he hadn't spoken.

Drew closed his eyes, knowing she wasn't going to give up, knowing that a part of him wanted—

needed—to tell her. Needed for her to understand what was at stake.

"We were on a stakeout," he said slowly, his voice rough. "We'd gotten a tip about one of Davis's warehouses."

He heard her quick indrawn breath as he said the name, but he didn't stop. She'd asked for the truth and she was going to get it.

"There was a coffee shop on the corner. We flipped a coin to see who'd go get coffee. I won. When I got back to the car, Martinez turned to say something to me. And then he was dead. The bullet that should have killed me went wide—maybe the shooter sneezed," he said, without humor. "It caught me in the leg instead of in the head."

"That's why you limp sometimes," she said, talking as much to herself as to him.

"That's why."

The motel room was silent while she absorbed his words. Drew could hear her breathing, a little too quick, as if his words had upset her. Good, he thought harshly. Let her be upset if it made her realize just what was at stake here.

"You're counting on me to destroy him, aren't you?" she said into the silence.

"Yes." He didn't add anything to soften the flat agreement. She was the best weapon he had, short of going after Davis with a shotgun himself. And this would be better in the end. Better to see Davis behind bars—the social position he'd so carefully cultivated stripped from him—than to see him dead.

Neither of them spoke again. Drew lay back against the pillows, his mind churning with old memories and new regrets. He shouldn't have said anything to her about the shooting. If it came out in court, he could be accused of tampering with the witness. Not that it mattered to him except that it could affect her testimony. Nothing mattered except bringing Davis down.

Kate lay staring into the darkness, digesting what Drew had told her. She'd known he wanted to see Lester Davis stopped, but she hadn't known that he had quite such a personal stake in it. His partner's murder, his own injury. He hungered for vengeance as much as justice.

And she was the key to both. She had to remember that. She was useful to him, and she'd be a fool to forget it.

Chapter Five

"This is where we'll be staying." Drew pulled the car up next to the curb in front of a small yellow house with a neatly fenced yard.

Kate looked from Drew to the house, her brows lifting in surprise. She wasn't sure what she'd been expecting, but this slice of small town suburbia wasn't it. The setting was much too... normal.

"Here?" she questioned, her disbelief obvious.

"Here. The neighbors should have the keys." He turned off the engine and then sat scowling at the little house. "They're expecting us."

"They are?" It was starting to occur to Kate that she'd been remiss in not asking for more details about the arrangements that had been made to protect her. She'd simply accepted Drew's assurance that she'd be safe. "Do they know what the situation is?"

"No." Drew seemed to hesitate and then slanted her an unreadable glance. "No one is to know why we're here."

"That makes sense." Kate unsnapped her seat belt and turned slightly in her seat to face him. "So what's our story?"

Drew didn't answer immediately. At least, not verbally. Reaching into his shirt pocket, he drew out a plain gold wedding band. Kate stared at it for a moment, her eyes wide and uncertain. It was the obvious cover, of course. They could have been brother and sister, but it wasn't as obvious a choice as being husband and wife.

She should have seen it coming when he'd insisted that they share a motel room. She *would* have seen it coming if she'd taken the trouble to look. But she'd been thinking about other things—like whether or not she'd ever get her life back again and the possibility that someone might be looking for her, wanting her dead. And the way Drew's rare smile made her stomach jump. She hadn't given nearly enough thought to the near future.

Held between Drew's thumb and forefinger, the ring gleamed dull gold in the sunlight. It was the most practical arrangement. That's all it was—pure practicality. It wasn't as if they were actually going to have to get married. The ring didn't mean a thing, really.

Which didn't explain the faint trembling of Kate's hand as she held it out. Drew hesitated and it occurred to her that she should have taken the ring from him and put it on herself, but it was already too late. He'd already taken her hand, his fingers strong and hard around hers as he slid the ring into place.

Their eyes met for an instant and it seemed—almost—as if something passed between them, something that sent an odd little shiver up Kate's spine. His fingers tightened over hers. Did he lean toward her or was it her imagination? And then he released her hand and reached for the door handle.

"Let me do most of the talking."

"All right." But she was talking to thin air. He was already out of the car.

Kate was aware of a slight unsteadiness of her hand as she pushed open her door. It was just the situation, she told herself. There was nothing to her reaction to Drew except the fact that she was dependent on him. It had been a long time since she'd been dependent on anyone else and it was bringing out a strange reaction in her. That's all it was.

IF SHE THOUGHT she'd gotten to know her companion during the past few days, Kate soon discovered how wrong she was. Standing on the concrete porch of the house next door to the one they'd be sharing, he seemed to change in some subtle way. His features relaxed, the taut lines easing from beside his mouth. His eyes softened, losing the hard edge that made her think of pale blue diamonds.

By the time the door opened in answer to the bell, the tough cop had disappeared and in his place was someone younger, more... ordinary. It could have been a different man entirely.

"Mrs. Dumont?" he asked the woman who pulled open the door and looked at them through the screen. "I'm Drew Ralston. This is my wife, Kate. We're renting the house next door. The Marsdens said we should get the key from you."

"Mr. Marsden called and said you'd be getting here today." The faint wariness in her eyes was replaced by friendly welcome. "Wait just a second and I ll get the key and take you over."

She was back in little more than the second she'd promised, pushing open the screen to join Kate and Drew on the porch. "You must be exhausted, driving all that way. I'm Jane, by the way. It's Janine, really, but everybody calls me Jane. I don't know why. Janine's a prettier name, don't you think?"

She didn't wait for an answer but swept by them and down the steps, her dark hair bouncing on the shoulders of her pale blue shirt.

"I think you'll like the neighborhood. It's pretty quiet, but everybody's friendly, too. We've been here almost fifteen years and we can't imagine living anywhere else. Did you drive straight through? I hope not. We drove all the way up the coast when Kenny—that's our son—was just a baby. Bill had to get back to work so we really didn't have a choice, but it was tiring. Do you plan on staying long?''

''We're not sure.'' It was Kate who responded when Drew didn't answer immediately. He'd been letting the words roll over him, paying little attention to them as they followed her down a sidewalk buckled by the roots of the elms that lined the street. Kate could hardly blame him for his inattention since, for a moment, it had seemed as if Jane Dumont could happily carry the conversation without any outside assistance.

''It all depends on how things go with my book,'' Drew added.

''Oh, you're a writer.'' Jane threw him a quick, speculative look over her shoulder as she led the way up the walk. ''Should I know your name?''

''Not yet. I'm taking a year off from teaching to write a novel.'' His smile managed to be both hopeful and a little self-deprecating. Kate didn't doubt that he could have called up a blush, if necessary.

''Well, you've picked a good place if you need peace and quiet.'' Jane started to slide the key into the lock, but Drew reached out to take it from her.

''This is our first real place together,'' he said, in answer to Jane's startled look. ''We'd sort of like to explore it alone, if you don't mind.''

Kate wondered if Jane heard the iron under the request or if she simply accepted his explanation at face value. Whichever it was, her startled look faded into an indulgent smile.

"Newlyweds. I'm not surprised. There's still a little of that starry-eyed look about the two of you."

More like an exhausted daze, Kate thought. But she did her best to look shy and bridal.

"I'll leave you two alone, then, but don't forget that I'm right next door if you need anything."

"Thank you, Jane." Drew gave her another of those wide open smiles that made Kate feel as if he was someone else entirely. She murmured her farewells as Jane's plump figure brushed past her and down the two steps to the cement walkway. She turned to watch the other woman, who paused at the sidewalk to smile back at them.

Behind her, she heard Drew mutter something uncomplimentary about friendly neighbors and then she gasped, barely swallowing a startled shriek as she felt herself being swept off her feet and lifted against his chest. Her arms came up automatically to circle his neck, her wide eyes meeting his.

"Newlyweds," he muttered by way of explanation and pushed open the door with his foot before carrying her over the threshold.

He set her down the moment the door shut behind them, stepping back so quickly that Kate might have been offended. At least, she might have been if she hadn't been occupied with controlling the odd flutter in the pit of her stomach.

"She was expecting me to carry you over the threshold," Drew said, as if she'd demanded an explanation.

"Of course." Kate looked at her hands and was annoyed to find them less than steady. She lifted her chin and forced herself to look at him. "Why newlyweds?"

"It helps explain any conflict in our stories. We can always pass it off as not having been married long enough to get the details straight."

"Of course." She cleared her throat, wishing she could think of a more intelligent response than just those two words. The truth was that it was starting to sink in on her that she was going to be sharing this house for an unknown length of time with a man she barely knew. A man who made her knees tremble and set butterflies in her stomach.

It was ironic, she thought. She'd left L.A. to escape one dangerous man...and ended up in the hands of another.

"I NEED THE CAR KEYS."

Drew lifted his eyes from the newspaper and gave Kate a questioning glance. "What for?"

"I need to get some things. I won't be gone long." She held out her hand and smiled.

"Give me a minute," Drew said. He snapped the paper shut. It was their first day in the house and he hadn't planned on doing anything more energetic than reading the paper, at least not before noon.

"You don't have to come with me," she protested as he stood. "I'm not going far."

"You don't go anywhere without me."

"You don't think Davis has killers lurking in town, do you?" Her tone was disbelieving.

"Probably not." He picked up his coffee cup and drained the last of its contents before rinsing the cup and setting it in the dishwasher. He'd been looking forward to a second cup, as well as a chance to read the paper at his leisure.

Kate had been right that first morning—he was *not* a morning person, not if he had a choice. It seemed like a real injustice that he had to protect a woman who woke up as chipper as a damned bird.

"I didn't want to drag you out," Kate was saying apologetically. "I really could go alone."

"No." He turned to look at her. "You don't go anywhere without me. Don't even walk next door without letting me know where you're going."

"But..."

"Nowhere, Kate." He interrupted her without apology. "I can't protect you if I don't know where you are."

"You don't think he'll find us here, do you?" Kate wrapped her arms around herself, unconsciously trying to hug away the chill his words had created.

"No, I don't. That's why Lavery sent us here."
He buried the urge to put his arms around her and
tell her not to worry, that there was nothing to
worry about. But there was a lot to worry about,
not least of which was his completely unprofessional and unwanted reaction to her.

"So you're just being extra cautious?" she suggested, looking a little less haunted.

"It's my job to be extra cautious. That's why I'm
here. That's what's going to keep you alive."

"I know." She gave him a quick smile. "I appreciate it. I don't know if I've said that, but I really do appreciate what you're doing for me."

Drew's fingers curled into his palms. He wanted
to taste that smile. He wanted to see if her mouth
could possibly be as soft as it looked.

"I'm doing my job," he said shortly, making it
clear that only a fool would read anything personal into his actions.

"I know." Kate flushed lightly, her eyes dropping away from his, and Drew felt as if he'd just
slapped a friendly puppy for no reason.

"I'll get the keys," he said gruffly.

WHEN SHE'D SAID she needed to go shopping, he'd
assumed she was talking about buying food, though
they'd stopped at a grocery store on their way to the
house the day before. Besides, if last night's dinner
was any indication, cooking was hardly one of

Kate's great loves and it certainly wasn't one of her talents.

He'd never realized that it was possible to cook hamburger to the actual consistency of concrete. But she'd proven it could be done and last night's meatballs could have been registered as weapons. He'd politely downed two of them and then waited until she went to bed to sneak back out to the kitchen to raid the refrigerator.

He felt a definite twinge of uneasiness at the thought that she planned to buy more food. If she could do that to hamburger, there was no telling what she could do to chicken. And he didn't really want to find out.

To his relief, Kate directed him to the discount store they'd passed on their way into town. At least she wasn't buying food. He parked the car and followed her into the store.

"I suppose you like blue," Kate said as she headed for the section marked Home Decor.

"I like it well enough," he admitted cautiously. What did his color preferences have to do with anything?

"Men always seem to like blue. Must be something genetic." She stopped in front of a display of throw pillows. "Here. These are perfect. They're bright and they're cheap."

"For what?"

"For the living room." She pulled two pillows out of the middle and Drew held his breath, wait-

ing to see the loosely piled mound tumble to the
floor. By some miracle, it stayed in place. "Hold
these, please."

He automatically took the pillows from her. She
circled the pile like a boxer looking for an opening
in an opponent's guard. She disappeared behind it
and he saw the pillows tremble as she yanked some
more free. When she came around the other side,
she was carrying four more pillows.

"Aren't these great?" she asked.

"I guess." He took two of the pillows from her.
He could only hope that he didn't have a sudden
need to draw his gun. Burdened as he was, if a bad
guy showed up, he'd probably have to bombard
him with pillows, rather than bullets. "Why are you
buying pillows for the living room?"

"Because it needs them." She seemed surprised
that he had to ask. "It's practically crying out for
a little color. Oh, look, they've got some vases on
sale."

"Oh." Drew didn't pursue the question. The living room hadn't said anything to him about needing color. In fact, none of the rooms had spoken to
him at all.

WITHIN A WEEK, Kate had transformed the empty
house into a home. The heavy curtains had been
drawn back from the multipaned windows. There
were vases filled with flowers in every room. The
pillows had been tossed on the sofa, lightening the

rather gloomy tweed fabric. Kate's quilting had taken up permanent residence in one corner of the small living room, adding bright colors and soft textures. The atmosphere was warm, cozy and welcoming.

Though he'd watched the transformation, even gone with Kate when she'd bought the pillows, Drew still found it hard to believe the change. Just as she'd done in the motels where they'd stayed, she'd somehow managed to turn a house into a home. It wasn't just the pillows or opening the curtains or rearranging the furniture. It was a subtle difference in the atmosphere, as though a gentle wind had blown through, sweeping away the staleness of the empty house and leaving something warm and vibrant in its place.

The change made him uncomfortable. Or maybe it was that it made him *too* comfortable. He found himself wanting to sink down on the sofa, pile the pillows behind his back, stretch his legs out and drowse the afternoon away. He had to remind himself that this was a job, not a vacation. The fact that he needed such a reminder annoyed him.

And the fact that Kate Sloane was creeping into his thoughts in a way that had nothing to do with her being a part of his job annoyed him even more.

"WHAT ARE YOU DOING?"

Kate looked over her shoulder, careful not to

move suddenly lest she lose her precarious balance on the chair.

"I'm measuring for curtains."

"What for?" Drew frowned at the window over the sink, seeing nothing wrong with the blinds that were there.

"Because the window needs something to soften it. The blinds are too hard by themselves." She turned back to the window, leaning forward to reach the window.

Drew's frown deepened as the movement tightened her jeans over her derriere. He curled his fingers into his palms, trying to ignore the urge to set his hands on those soft curves.

Kate was vividly aware of Drew standing behind her, watching her. The knowledge made her fingers tremble and her knees feel slightly rubbery. A ridiculous reaction, she scolded herself. Other than her value to him as a witness, Drew Hunter probably didn't even know she was alive.

Exasperated with herself, Kate leaned toward the window, her movements quick as she sought to distract herself from her thoughts. She gasped as the chair shifted beneath her, edging backward slightly. It couldn't have moved more than an inch, but it was enough to make her grab for the edge of the counter, her heart bumping with sudden fright.

An instant later, her heart bumped again, not exactly with fright as she felt Drew's hands close over her hips. The firm grip steadied her balance even as it unraveled her nerves.

"You're going to get yourself killed if you don't look out."

"Wouldn't it be funny if you brought me all this way to keep me safe, only to have me break my neck measuring a window?" Since Drew showed no signs of releasing her as long as she was perched on the chair and the feel of his hands was too disturbing to ignore, Kate stepped down and turned to look at him.

"I don't know why you're doing all this work, anyway. This isn't your home. It's just a place you're staying for a little while."

"I spent most of my childhood in places where I was just 'staying for a little while.'" Her full mouth curved in a smile of slightly sad remembrance. "It sometimes seemed like my mother and I moved on a daily basis. I learned to make homes wherever we stopped, even if it was only for a few days. To put down a few roots."

"Why put down roots if you know they're going to be yanked up?" Drew asked, thinking of his own unsettled childhood and how he'd learned never to allow roots to grow, never to give in to the urge to think of any place as home.

"You can't survive without roots," Kate said softly, her eyes searching.

"Better to keep them inside yourself, then," he said, his voice harsher than he'd intended.

"Is that what you do? Try to keep them all inside?" Kate's expression was thoughtful as she considered the idea. She shook her head slowly. "It sounds very lonely, I think."

"It's a lot more comfortable," Drew snapped, aware that she'd touched a nerve. "Here, if you're determined to put up new curtains, let me do the measuring."

Kate wrote down the measurements he gave her, but her thoughts weren't on the curtains anymore. She was wondering what had happened in his life to make him guard himself so carefully, holding everything inside.

"Let me know when you want to go get the curtains," he said as he stepped down from the chair. "Remember, you're not to go out alone."

"I remember." Though she thought the precaution unnecessary since she couldn't see how Lester Davis could have tracked her this far, Kate didn't argue. It was Drew's job to protect her. She'd accept his judgment on how to go about it.

When the measurements were complete, Drew set down the measuring tape and started to leave. He hesitated in the doorway and turned back to her, looking at her with an unreadable expression. Warning? Concern? Impatience?

"This isn't real, Kate. Don't lose sight of that."

"I won't."

She hoped Drew accepted her reassurance. She wasn't sure she believed it herself. The past few days, it had been incredibly easy to forget the reason she was here. Los Angeles and Lester Davis and the possibility of testifying seemed a very long way away.

Kate turned and leaned her arms on the counter as she looked out the window at the backyard. How many times had she fantasized about having a house like this in a peaceful little town, with a window over the kitchen sink that looked out on a view of flower beds and sweet, green grass?

During all the many moves she and her mother had made, they'd lived in houses only a time or two. Mostly Belinda had preferred apartments. Less upkeep, less to leave behind, she'd say when the question of a house came up. Kate had accepted her decision, just as she'd accepted all her mother's decisions. But in her heart, she'd dreamed of a time when she'd stay in one place for more than a few months, a place where she'd put down strong, solid roots that wouldn't be torn loose by someone else's restless urge to travel.

A house that looked something like this one. There was even the white picket fence of her childish fantasies, she thought ruefully. How could she help but fall just a little in love with the place?

And the man who shared it with her?

She winced away from that question, afraid to look at it too directly. As Drew had pointed out, this was all pretend. It wouldn't do to forget that. It was one thing to play at keeping house, but she couldn't afford to lose sight of reality. And the reality was that Drew was here to protect her and he was only doing that because it was his job, because he had a personal stake in seeing that she lived to testify.

This isn't real, Kate.

She closed her eyes as she heard the echo of his warning. No, it wasn't real, but she was very much afraid that she was starting to wish it were.

BY THE END of a week and a half, Drew was starting to feel like a tiger in a ruffle-trimmed cage.

There'd been no word from Lavery. No word about how long it might be before Drew could return Kate Sloane to L.A. and get out of her life. And the disturbing thing was that, deep down, he was afraid that he wasn't in as much of a hurry to do that as he should have been.

A month ago, if someone had suggested that he could spend more than an hour in a town with only one main street, sharing a house with a woman he didn't know, living like a typical, suburban husband and that he wouldn't be climbing the walls with boredom, Drew would have told them that they were crazy.

But here he was, and it wasn't boredom that had him climbing the walls. He only wished it were.

He stood near the window of the room that had been set aside as his office. Since he was supposed to be writing a book, a computer sat squarely in the middle of the desk. He turned it on when he came into the room, but the only time he touched the keyboard was to play solitaire or blackjack. Most of the hours he was in the room were spent reading.

Or simply avoiding Kate.

And that was a hell of a thing to admit. He was a grown man, an experienced police officer, and he was all but barricading himself in a ten-by-ten room to avoid spending time with the witness he was protecting. And it wasn't even because he disliked her company. If that had been the reason, he would have shrugged it off as a part of the job. The problem was that he found himself wanting to seek out her company, looking for reasons to talk to her, to see her. And that scared the hell out of him.

He stared out the window at the slender figure kneeling next to one of the neglected rosebushes. What was it about her? He'd known women more beautiful, more sophisticated. None of them had lingered in his thoughts past the moment he left their company.

Kate braced one hand in the dirt and stretched forward, reaching for a weed that was trying to hide behind the rose. The movement made her T-shirt ride up, baring a palm's width of pale skin between waistband and hem. If he were really her husband, he'd have every right to go out there and put his hand on that innocently exposed skin. He could slide his fingers beneath her shirt, exploring the length of her spine. She'd arch into his touch like a sleek little cat, turning her head to look at him, her eyes all green and hungry. They'd come into the house and . . .

Aware that his jeans were suddenly much too tight, Drew cursed and spun away from the window. What the hell was the matter with him? Standing here, fantasizing about the woman he was supposed to be protecting. She should be nothing more than a package to him, no different than if he were protecting a valuable statue.

So what if her eyes crinkled at the corners when she smiled. What difference did it make that she created a home wherever she went. If he'd wanted a home, he'd have stayed married, right? He'd have been willing to give up his job if that's what it took to make Diane happy. If there was one thing he'd learned from his childhood, it was that there were few things more ephemeral, more easily taken away, than a home.

Drawn against his will, Drew turned back to the window. Kate was sitting back on her heels, holding out her hand to the scruffy gray cat who lived next door. At least, he lived next door now. Kate had found the cat when they went out to buy some food one day. He'd been scrounging through a trash can and her heart had immediately gone out to him.

Remembering the incident with the dog, Drew hadn't wasted his breath arguing with her when she'd said that the cat was coming home with them—she'd find him a home. And she had. Since Jane Dumont and her family had two large dogs, Kate had introduced herself to the elderly man who lived on the other side of them and suggested that he might like to adopt a cat.

Remembering the old man's surprised expression, Drew felt his mouth curve.

"I've never had a pet," he'd told her in the tone of someone who was quite content to continue that way.

"Oh, how sad." Kate's eyes filled with quick tears. "Then you'll be so glad to have Sammy." She thrust the huge gray cat into his arms. "He'll be such a wonderful companion."

Drew, who'd been standing on the sidelines, waited to see the big tom prove his companionable nature by clawing his new owner. To his surprise, Sammy, who must have been smarter than he looked, immediately rubbed his scarred head against the old man's hand and began purring loudly.

"He knows he's going to be happy with you," Kate said happily.

"But, I..." Mr. Waterman looked down at the cat as if he wasn't sure how he'd come to be holding it. "I don't know what to do with a cat," he said plaintively.

"Oh, cats practically take care of themselves. We bought a litter pan and some litter and a bag of food and a cat dish for him."

Drew set the bag containing those items on the porch and gave Mr. Waterman a sympathetic look. The man was doomed. There was no way he wasn't taking the cat. Between them, Kate and Sammy had him beat.

"I don't know, Mrs. Ralston. I've never had a pet." Sammy butted his chin against the old man's hand, who automatically began scratching behind one torn ear.

"Sammy will let you know what he needs," Kate said. She reached out to give Sammy a pat on the head. Sammy turned his big yellow eyes on her and blinked indifferently. He obviously understood which side his future bread was buttered on. He began to knead his paws against Mr. Waterman's arm. "See, he loves you already."

"Well, I suppose a cat... They're not a great deal of trouble, after all." He was going down for the third time, still floundering but sinking rapidly. "It's not as if it were a dog."

Drew didn't doubt that Kate could have persuaded him to take in a full-grown Great Dane if she'd decided that they were made for each other.

"Maybe he would make a nice companion," he said weakly, giving up the battle.

"He'll be a wonderful companion, Mr. Waterman. I thought of you as soon as I saw him."

Drew wondered what it was in the battle-scarred gray tom that had reminded her of the neat-as-a-pin retired bank clerk, but he decided it was better not to ask.

"Yes, well, thank you, Mrs. Ralston." He still looked faintly surprised by his agreement.

He didn't seem to regret the decision. Several times since then, Drew had seen him sitting on the front porch, the gray cat settled on his lap, looking quite content.

Kate's fingers stroked over the gray fur, less tattered looking than it had been a week ago. The cat leaned into her hand, and Drew found himself envying the animal his freedom to enjoy Kate's touch.

He realized the direction his thoughts were heading and spun away from the window, his dark brows hooking together in a frown. "You're losing it, Hunter. You're jealous of a cat, for God's sake! And you're talking to yourself."

He thrust his fingers through his hair and glared at the silent telephone. "When are you going to call, Lavery?"

But there was a part of him that didn't want Lavery to call because it would mean an end to the pretend world in which they were living. The thought was enough to send him out of the den and then out of the house.

It was a beautiful day, full of sunshine and singing birds. Drew paused on the edge of the front porch, glaring at the blue sky and the bright splash of poppies that grew near the corner of the house. If Norman Rockwell had been a Californian, he probably would have painted Hayfield. All pretty houses and neat lawns and flower beds.

Where was concrete and smog when you needed it? Drew wondered sourly. Still frowning, he strode down the walkway and turned onto the sidewalk. He needed to get away for a while, even if it was only for a few minutes. He was spending too much time sitting in his "office" with nothing to do but think. Too much thinking could be hazardous.

"Hi, Mr. Ralston."

Drew slowed his stride and smiled at the teenager, slipping instantly into the skin of history teacher-budding writer-friendly neighbor. Kenny Dumont was almost fifteen and at a stage in his growth where he seemed to be all arms and legs.

"Hi, Kenny. No school today?"

"Nah. Some kinda teachers' conference." As he spoke, he continued to absently bounce the basketball he held, the thunk of leather hitting the concrete drive punctuating his speech.

"Great weather for a day off," Drew commented, preparing to move on.

"Yeah. 'Cept Mom won't let me have anybody over cause I ditched a test last week. One dumb old math test and I'm grounded for a week." It was obvious that he thought the punishment much too harsh for the crime. He slanted Drew a look of blended defiance and guilt. "I guess you think that kind of thing is important, huh? Bein' a teacher and all."

"Actually, math was my worst subject," Drew admitted. "I ditched a test or two myself."

"Yeah?" Kenny brightened. "And you graduated, right?"

"Yes. But I spent a couple of years in summer school to do it. And it's a lot tougher to get into college these days than it was twenty years ago. You need to keep your grades up."

"That's what Mom and Dad keep telling me," Kenny said, his tone glum. Clearly he was disappointed to have their point of view corroborated.

"I hate to say it, but they're right." Drew tried to sound properly regretful, forcing the amusement from his voice.

"You play basketball?" Kenny apparently decided to abandon the unsatisfactory topic of school.

"In high school."

"You want to play a little one-on-one?" The boy's voice was both uncertain and hopeful.

Drew opened his mouth to refuse politely. "Won't your mom object? You're grounded, right?"

"She won't mind. She just doesn't want me seeing my friends."

And since he wasn't a friend, it had to be all right, Drew thought, amused. Not that he was going to play basketball with the kid, of course. He was in no mood for company. Especially not fourteen-year-old-kid company. He just wanted to take a brisk walk and get his thoughts in order.

"I haven't played in a long time," he said.

"That's okay. I'll go easy on you." There was brash challenge in Kenny's grin, his dark eyes sparkling with anticipation.

Of course, he wasn't going to accept that challenge. He'd smile and refuse. Playing basketball with the neighbor's kid was hardly essential to maintaining his cover. Which didn't explain how he came to be walking up the driveway. Or the rush of pure competition he felt when Kenny thrust the ball into his hands.

"Since you're an old dude, I'll give you first shot."

"You may live to regret that," Drew said, grinning recklessly.

ALMOST AN HOUR LATER, Drew pushed open the front door and stepped into the cool interior of the house. He was hot, sweaty and exhausted. And for the first time in weeks, completely relaxed. He rolled his shoulders, enjoying the pull of overworked muscles.

He'd forgotten how much energy it took to play basketball. And what Kenny lacked in experience was more than compensated for by his youth. Had *he* ever had that much energy, Drew wondered, his mouth curving in a half smile. The kid had run him ragged. It had taken every bit of half-forgotten skill he'd ever had to manage to hold his own. He'd done it, but he had a feeling that his muscles were going to punish him for it tomorrow. At least he no longer felt as if he were going to explode.

He started away from the door and stopped abruptly, his eyes meeting Kate's. Coming in from the bright sunlight, he hadn't seen her standing in the hallway just a few feet away, a glass of ice tea in her hand.

KATE HAD STOPPED, startled by his abrupt entrance. Out the window, she'd seen him playing basketball with Kenny. She'd stood there, mesmerized by the quick movements of his body, watching the play of muscles under his thin T-shirt. It had taken a considerable exercise of will to force herself to turn away from the window and go back to her gardening.

It had taken even more willpower to stay away from that same window when she came in again. Now she wished she'd given in to temptation. At least then she wouldn't have been so completely unprepared to come face-to-face with him.

Their eyes met and then Kate's dropped to his bare chest. He must have taken his T-shirt off partway through the game and now it dangled from his hand. It wasn't the first time she'd seen his chest. Certainly when he'd burst out of the motel bathroom to save her from the pizza boy, he'd been wearing less. It wasn't as if she hadn't seen him before, she reminded herself.

But that didn't prevent her mouth from going dry or the sudden increase of her pulse. Her fingers tightened around the icy glass. She wanted to cross the few feet that separated them and lay her palms against that mat of black hair and feel the muscles beneath. The strength of the urge was almost frightening and she jerked her eyes upward, staring at Drew's face.

Drew read the hunger in her gaze and felt his whole body tighten in reaction. All the tension he'd thought worked off by the basketball game was suddenly back, increased tenfold. It was one thing to know he wanted Kate. He was accustomed to suppressing his own needs and desires. But to see his own hunger reflected in her eyes...

His hand tightened over the T-shirt as sexual tension became an almost living, breathing presence between them. He had only to cover the short distance that separated them and pull her into his arms and she wouldn't offer even a whisper of protest.

He knew it.

She knew it.

What was worse, she wanted him to do just that. He could read it in her eyes. And God knew, she couldn't want it any more than he did.

So why not do it? The small, sly voice whispered in his mind, nudging him toward what could only be disaster.

With a mutter that could have been either curse or greeting, Drew moved away from the door. Kate caught her breath and braced herself for his touch, knowing she should push him away.

Knowing she'd pull him closer.

But he brushed past her, striding down the hall and disappearing into his bedroom, the door shutting with a decisive click behind him.

For a moment, she stood exactly where she was, feeling her knees tremble. She closed her eyes, wanting to believe that what she felt was relief.

And knowing it was disappointment.

Chapter Six

Neither Drew nor Kate mentioned the incident in the hallway. After all, there was really nothing to talk about, right? They hadn't spoken, hadn't touched, hadn't done anything out of the ordinary. So they'd exchanged a glance. And it had seemed, for a moment, as if that glance contained enough heat to melt paint off the walls.

But it had probably been her imagination, Kate told herself.

He was spending too much time thinking, Drew thought. He was starting to imagine things.

They were scrupulously polite. And each was careful to spend as little time as possible with the other.

Drew spent an hour or so most afternoons playing basketball with Kenny, telling himself that he was doing it because he wanted to keep in shape, because it strengthened his injured leg. It had nothing to do with the need to work off tension.

Kate spent a lot of time in the garden and she was extremely careful to avoid the entryway when there was any chance that Drew might be coming in after playing ball, his shirt off, his torso sun warmed and damp with sweat. Not that she cared what his torso looked like, she told herself. She'd barely even noticed it.

If there was any attraction between them at all, it was just a case of propinquity or familiarity breeding lust. That's all it could possibly be. That's all she'd *let* it be.

IT WAS TWO DAYS after the nonincident in the hallway that Kate didn't get up for breakfast. Since she hadn't been kidding when she'd told him she was a morning person, Drew was surprised to find the kitchen empty when he wandered out for a cup of coffee.

He added water and coffee to the coffeemaker, sure that Kate would come stumbling out any minute, surprised that the coffee wasn't already made since she usually made it. It was about the only thing he could safely let her do in the kitchen. She might be a whiz at sewing and gardening, but she was the worst cook he'd ever seen.

As much out of self-defense as out of desire for a fair division of labor, the cooking had become his job. In a way, she'd chosen him for it that first night, when she'd told him to cook dinner in her apartment. The memory made Drew smile, remembering his annoyance at her peremptory order.

Kate still hadn't appeared by the time the coffee was ready. Drew poured himself a cup and sipped it, savoring the silence. It was so peaceful without Kate's usual morning chatter. Nothing to hear but the birds perched in the old maple outside the back door.

Drew took another sip of coffee and frowned out the window at the early-spring morning. It was nice to be up like this, alone. In the quiet. He could drink his coffee in peace for a change. It felt great. Really, really great.

He glanced over his shoulder, his ears tuned for any sound from the direction of Kate's room. But there was nothing. Just the silence. That wonderful silence. The silence that was beginning to feel downright oppressive, he admitted.

Setting his cup on the counter, Drew left the kitchen. The fact was, he'd gotten used to her talking his ear off every morning. It didn't matter what she said. It didn't even really matter if he listened. He was just used to the sound of her voice. Later, he'd think about what a bad sign *that* was. At the moment, he wanted to make sure she was all right.

He stood outside her bedroom door for a moment, listening. If she was sleeping in, he was going to look like an idiot if he woke her. On the other hand, if something had happened to her...

Like what, Hunter?

Like she could have fallen and hurt herself.

So badly that she couldn't even call for help?

It was possible.

God, now he was starting to carry on arguments with himself! Next thing he knew, he'd start *losing* the argument.

This assignment was going to be the death of him. Or at least the death of his sanity. Drew thrust his fingers through his hair and glared at the blank door. He'd just about talked himself into going back to his coffee when he heard Kate cough.

He tapped on the door. "Kate?"

"Go away."

She sounded . . . odd.

"Are you okay?"

"I'm fine." She didn't sound fine. Drew hesitated. He could just take her word for it and go away as she'd told him to. But she didn't sound right. She didn't sound like Kate. On the other hand, what could be wrong? He'd checked the house out and installed his own simple but effective security system. There was no way someone could have gotten in to hold her hostage in her bedroom.

Still frowning, he turned away from the door. Maybe she just felt like being alone. It was his job to protect her, not to interpret her moods.

He'd taken only a step or two when there was a solid crash from the room behind him, followed by a muffled string of words that didn't bear repeating. He turned back, setting one palm flat against the door, the fingers of the other circling the knob.

"Kate? What's wrong?"

"Nothing. Go away." The command was somewhat weakened by the fit of coughing that ended it.

"You sound like hell. I'm coming in." Without giving her time to argue any further, he pushed open the door and stepped inside.

It was the first time he'd been in the room since the day they'd arrived. It had been bad enough to know that she was sleeping just a few feet down the hallway without being able to picture exactly what the room looked like.

Like the rest of the house, Kate's bedroom had a feeling of having been lived in, of being a home. Maybe it was the glass eyes of the small teddy bear that stared at him from the dresser or the casual way she'd looped the curtains back, framing the sunny green vista of the backyard. Maybe it was the jeans draped over the foot of the bed or the tennis shoes that sat next to the closet, their toes at crazy angles to each other.

It was nothing and everything. It was Kate. It was what drew him to her even as his instincts said he should back away. But at the moment, he was less interested in the decor than he was in the room's occupant.

Kate sat in the middle of the bed, her pillows a rumpled mound behind her, her hair a tangled mass on her shoulders, her face flushed with annoyance.

On the floor beside the bed was a plastic pitcher, a broken glass and a damp spot on the carpet that was, presumably, the contents of the glass.

"What happened?"

"I dropped a glass," she snapped. "Is that illegal?"

"No." Drew's brows lifted at her uncharacteristic grouchiness. "I'll clean up the glass before you step on it."

"I can do that." But he was already beside the bed, crouching down to pick up the pieces of broken glass.

Kate watched in silence, pulling the covers closer around her shoulders. He stood and tossed the glass into the trash.

"I'll get the vacuum."

"Don't worry about it."

"There are bound to be glass chips in the carpet."

"I doubt the carpet minds."

Drew didn't bother to comment but left, returning a moment later with the vacuum. Kate didn't speak again until he'd vacuumed the area to his satisfaction and reached down to turn off the machine. The silence it left behind seemed painfully loud.

Kate sniffled discreetly into a tissue, hoping Drew was too busy winding the cord into place to notice.

"Thank you," she said when he straightened and looked at her. She tried to look dignified, which wasn't easy when she was sitting in bed, her hair uncombed, and wearing a red football jersey with a white number one emblazoned across the chest.

"I appreciate the help." She hoped he'd take the words as dismissal and go away, leaving her to suffer in private. The last thing she wanted was to have him standing there, looking at her with those pale blue eyes that seemed capable of seeing right through her.

The silence stretched and she shifted uneasily, wishing she could get up and stalk into the bathroom, dignity intact. Unfortunately the football jersey barely covered her thighs and she wasn't entirely sure her knees could be depended on to support her for a casual stroll, let alone a proper walk. She settled for lifting her chin an inch and doing her best to look impatient.

"You look like hell," Drew said bluntly, destroying her faint hope that the light was dim enough to conceal her red nose.

"Thank you." The intended sarcasm was somewhat muffled by the sneeze that forced her to bury her nose in a tissue. The first sneeze was followed by two more in quick succession, and by the time the fit had ended Kate was incapable of offering more than a weak glare in his direction as she leaned back against the pillows.

"How long have you been sick?" Drew asked, looking less than sympathetic.

"I started feeling it yesterday afternoon. But I'm not really sick." She proved the statement by coughing.

"You should have gone to bed as soon as you started feeling bad."

"I wanted to finish planting the flowers Jane gave us," she muttered.

"Why? We're probably not even going to be here to see the damn things bloom." His tone was sharper than he'd intended, edged by concern.

"I couldn't leave them in those pots. They were suffocating."

"Fine. And you're sick."

"I'm not sick because of the plants," she snapped, feeling her eyes sting with the threat of tears. She blinked rapidly, annoyed by her own weakness.

"I didn't mean to snarl," Drew said, his tone gentling. Illogically Kate felt even more like crying.

"I'm sorry I snapped," she offered in return, hoping he'd attribute her watery eyes to the cold.

"You're flushed." He reached out to put his hand on her forehead and the feel of his cool touch on her hot skin made Kate want to cry again. "You feel warm."

"I feel like hell," she said, finding a certain relief in admitting it.

"Maybe you should see a doctor." He let his hand fall to his side and frowned down at her.

"It's just a cold." He continued to frown and Kate drew the covers higher over her shoulders, huddling under them. "Don't worry, Drew. I'm not going to die before you get me to court."

"That wasn't what I was thinking of," he said stiffly and Kate was immediately ashamed of her peevishness.

"I know. I'm sorry." She reached out and caught his hand when he started to step away. "Colds always make me crabby."

He hesitated a moment and then his hand relaxed in hers, his mouth curving in a faint smile. "Like mornings make me?"

A stuffy head and a fever were not enough to completely muffle the effect of that smile. Kate felt her heart bump against her breastbone and hoped he'd attribute her sudden flush to her cold.

THERE WAS, DREW SOON discovered, no way to nurse someone through a cold and still maintain your distance from them. If Kate had simply developed a sniffle, he could have offered his sympathy and stayed out of her way. But she quickly developed enough symptoms to qualify for a cold-tablet commercial.

It wasn't that she asked for help. Far from it. But it would have taken a harder heart than his own to simply ignore her misery. And if the thought strayed in that he couldn't ignore Kate, with or without a cold, Drew pushed it aside. He was just doing his job. Okay, so his job description didn't exactly say anything about making chicken soup and squeezing oranges, but he *was* supposed to take care of her.

For Kate's part, she was just grateful for the hot soup, cold juice and unending supply of tissues. Who would have thought that Drew Hunter—Mr. Taciturn himself—would turn out to make such a mean bowl of soup? When she commented on it, he shrugged.

"Your taste buds aren't at their best," he pointed out. "I don't think you'd qualify as a discerning critic, at the moment."

But she thought he looked pleased and she found that small touch of vanity oddly endearing, evidence that he was human, no matter how much he tried to conceal the fact. Not that she'd had any real doubts about his humanity. It was just that her illness was providing more proof of it. In fact, it might almost be possible to enjoy being sick just for the pleasure of having Drew hover over her.

"BOARDWALK! OH, NO." Kenny's voice descended into something perilously close to a whine. "Come on, Kate. You could let me off the hook, just this one time, couldn't you? You don't need the money," he pointed out, looking at the stacks of colorful bills in front of her.

"It's the principle of the thing," Kate told him. "If I let you off this time, what about the next time? And what do I tell my other tenants?'' She gave him a look that managed to contain both impossible virtue and out-and-out greed. "Pay up."

Kenny looked at Drew, but he could only offer a sympathetic shrug as he reached for the dice to take his own turn. He'd never have believed that sweet, sympathetic Kate would turn out to have the soul of a Wall Street banker when it came to Monopoly. The woman had a talent for buying property and hanging on to it, not to mention the luck of the devil.

He shook the dice absently in one hand as he watched her transact her business with Kenny. It was a good thing she'd nearly cleaned both him and Kenny out, he thought. This was her first full day out of bed and she was starting to look a little pale. It had taken a week to get her to this point. He didn't want her staying up much longer and risking a relapse.

It struck him suddenly that he was thinking very much like a husband. He frowned down at the meager stack of play money in front of him. It was his job, of course. He was supposed to take care of her, to make sure that she was safe and well. But there were moments lately when he suspected that his feelings for Kate weren't as strictly professional as he'd have liked.

"Are you trying to shake the spots off?" Kate's polite inquiry brought Drew's eyes up and made him realize that he was still shaking the dice.

"I'm thinking about my next move," he told her coolly before tossing the dice onto the board. Six spots stared up at him.

"Oooh, good move! Marvin Gardens with two hotels." Kate's voice dripped with gleeful avarice. "Let's see how much you owe me."

Drew exchanged a long-suffering look with Kenny. "She's been sick," Kenny said, shaking his head sadly. "That's why we gotta let her win."

"Let me win? Ha! You just can't admit that you've been beaten by superior skill." She stared down her nose at them, looking so adorably smug that Drew had the sudden urge to lean across the table and kiss her. But he supposed that would embarrass Kenny so he settled for reaching out to tug a lock of silky hair.

"Pride goes before a fall," he warned her.

"It's not pride. It's simply an unbiased assessment of my superior Monopoly-playing ability." Her expression was so exaggeratedly haughty that Drew couldn't repress a grin. Damn, she was cute.

It was only much later that it occurred to him that, for a few minutes, he'd completely forgotten that this was all a game of pretend, that he and Kate weren't really husband and wife.

The doorbell rang just as Kate announced the outrageous rental fee that Drew owed her.

"Probably my mom," Kenny said, glancing over his shoulder with a hunted look. "I told her I'd take out the trash. Tell her I'll be home in a few minutes, would you?'' He gave Drew a pleading look. ''Kate's bound to land on one of my properties this time around.''

''I'll tell her.'' Drew pushed back his chair and stood, choosing not to point out that Baltic Avenue with one house was hardly likely to make a dent in the fortune Kate had amassed. ''Pay her for me, would you?'' He shoved his small stack of bills in Kenny's direction and went to answer the door.

Behind him, he could hear Kenny arguing that her rent was excessive and asking had she ever heard of the term ''slum lord.'' He shook his head. The kid was probably going to make a hell of a lawyer some day. He was still smiling as he pulled open the door, expecting to see Jane's exasperated face.

But it wasn't Jane. The man standing on the porch was about Drew's height but outweighed him by fifty pounds. His round features and the shock of curling red hair that was starting to inch its way back from his forehead gave him a look of friendly innocence. He looked as if he should be growing wheat somewhere in Kansas or running a café named Mom's. What he didn't look like was a cop, which was part of what made him a good one.

Drew's smile vanished as if it had never existed, the lingering warmth fading from his eyes, leaving them glacial blue.

''Murphy.'' There was no welcome in the greeting. Just flat acknowledgment.

"Ralston." The other man's round face split in a grin as he thrust out his hand. "Hope you don't mind me dropping by like this. I was in the area and remembered this was where you'd said you were going to be staying while you were writing your great American novel. Thought you might welcome a little news from your old stomping grounds."

Drew took his hand, forcing a smile that didn't even approach his eyes. If anyone happened to be watching, it would simply look like two old acquaintances greeting each other. In a way that's exactly what they were. He'd never worked directly with Dave Murphy, but he knew him by reputation. His reputation was that he was a good cop, one who couldn't be bought at any price.

He wasn't surprised that Lavery had chosen Murphy to act as contact. What did surprise him was the fierce wave of resentment he felt at the other man's presence. But now was not the time to analyze that resentment.

"Come in." He stepped back to let Murphy enter the hallway.

"Nice little place you got here," Murphy said.

"Yes." Drew's flat response was not encouraging. "We can talk in my office." But to get to the office, they had to pass the living room and it would look odd if he didn't stop.

"I don't think you've met my wife," he said as they stopped in the doorway. Later he'd consider how easily the words "my wife" had come to him. "And this is our neighbor's son, Kenny. This is Dave Murphy, Kate. An old colleague of mine."

Kenny acknowledged the introduction and returned his attention to the Monopoly board, his expression glum. Kate rose, her eyes fixed on Drew, holding both fear and questions. She didn't know Murphy, of course, but she knew, as Kenny didn't, that a "colleague" of Drew's was not a history teacher.

"You'll have to finish without me," Drew said with a tight smile.

"Of course." Kate's smile was tense around the edges, her eyes anxious as she watched them leave. Drew wanted to offer her reassurance, but he had none to give.

"Never thought I'd see Drew Hunter playing Monopoly," Murphy said as soon as the door of the den shut behind them.

"Why did Lavery send you?" Drew asked, ignoring the comment. Stopping in front of the desk, he turned to look at Murphy.

Murphy's brows rose slightly at Drew's abrupt tone, but he chose not to comment. Without waiting for an invitation—perhaps sensing that it wouldn't be forthcoming—he settled himself in the room's one chair.

"Since I was heading this way to go fishing at my brother's place in Oregon, Lavery figured there'd be no reason for anyone to question my going. He asked me to stop by and update you."

"And..." Drew saw no reason to conceal his impatience.

"And Davis is looking for her." He jerked his head in the direction of the living room.

Though it was no more than he'd been expecting, Drew felt the words strike him with the force of a physical blow. "How long?"

Murphy shrugged. "Since right after you left. He was suspicious, and when she disappeared he must have figured she had a reason."

"What does he know?"

"Not much. Just that she's gone. Since Lavery spirited you off like this, there isn't much Davis *can* know. Rumor is, the lieutenant has taken a lot of heat on this one."

"He can handle it." Drew wasn't worried about Lavery. He'd known what he was doing when he set this up, and even if it ended up costing him his job, he wouldn't cave in to pressure from above to reveal their whereabouts. The man was pure steel.

"There ain't much he can't handle," Murphy agreed. "He wants you to stay put. Says you're not to call in unless it's an emergency and that he'll be in touch when they're ready for you to bring the witness back to L.A."

Drew was surprised by the flash of annoyance he felt at hearing Kate called "the witness." She was a person, dammit, not a chess piece.

"Never thought I'd see you playing Monopoly," Murphy said again. He studied Drew as if seeing him for the first time. "Domesticity seems to suit you, Hunter."

"It's all part of the cover," Drew said, his tone repressive. The fact was that playing Monopoly with the neighbors' son could hardly be labeled an essential part of maintaining their cover. They could simply have established themselves as a couple with little interest in neighborly relations.

Or they could have if Kate hadn't been the kind of person she was. Drew doubted that she could be reserved if her life depended on it. *And it very well might,* he thought grimly.

MURPHY DIDN'T STAY long. Having delivered the message that Lavery wanted Drew and Kate to continue as they were until he contacted them, he made his departure, continuing on his trip to Oregon. The side journey had cost him so little time that, even if someone were to be around to note his arrival at his brother's fishing shack, they'd have no reason to think he might have made a detour.

The house was quiet when the two men left the den. The Monopoly game had been returned to its box and Kenny had gone home, presumably to attend to the trash he'd neglected earlier. Kate was not in sight, but Drew knew she must be wondering what Murphy had said, wondering what his arrival might mean to her future.

Drew shut the door behind the other man, but didn't immediately go in search of her. He stood in the hallway for a minute, trying to sort out his own tangled thoughts.

He'd nearly managed to forget the reason he was here, he thought. He'd been sitting there, playing silly games and, for a little while, the pretend had seemed like reality. Before Murphy showed up, he hadn't been thinking like a cop. He'd been thinking like a history teacher, turned would-be writer, with nothing more to worry about than whether a throw of the dice was going to land a little metal shoe on Boardwalk.

And his first emotion on seeing Murphy hadn't been concern or even question. It had been a stab of bitter resentment at the sudden reminder that the cozy little domestic scene was all pretend.

What the hell was happening to him?

But there was no answer to that question. Or at least none he was willing to accept.

KATE HEARD DREW ENTER the kitchen behind her, but she didn't immediately turn. She wasn't sure she wanted to see his expression, was even less sure she wanted to hear what their visitor had had to say. She continued to stir the milk she was heating for cocoa, watching the swirl of motion as if it demanded every bit of her concentration.

They'd been doing just fine, she thought fiercely, aware that Drew was watching her. Sometimes she didn't even think about why they were here. There'd even been a few moments when it had almost been possible to believe that it was all real.

"Davis is looking for you."

It took a moment for the quiet words to reach her and then the spoon clattered onto the stove top. Kate didn't turn to look at him, staring instead at the droplets of milk, hardly visible against the white enamel. One sentence and her pretend life was suddenly full of cracks.

"Does he know where I am?" She was surprised by the evenness of her voice, surprised to see that her hand was steady as she reached out to pick up a dishcloth.

"No."

"That's good, isn't it?" She wiped the milk from the stove before finally turning to look at him, her features set in a look of calm acceptance.

"It's good." Drew was leaning against the counter, but Kate could almost feel the tension in him, belying his casual stance.

"Good." She turned back to the stove, staring at the pan of milk without seeing it, trying not to think, trying not to feel.

"If he finds me, he's going to kill me, isn't he?" It was the first time she'd actually said the words out loud.

"He's not going to find you," Drew said roughly.

"But if he did, he'd kill me." It was no longer a question. It was a statement of fact and she heard confirmation in Drew's silence.

Kate reached for the pan of milk and then drew her hand back when she saw that it was no longer steady. Though she'd been living with it for weeks now, the idea that someone actually wanted her dead was nearly impossible to grasp.

"He'd have to go through me to get to you, Kate." Drew's words were intended to reassure, but instead, they conjured up an immediate image of him lying on the ground, life drained from him. And all because of her.

Kate crossed her arms at her waist, feeling a chill that had nothing to do with the temperature of the room. When they'd arrived here, she'd made up her mind to forget the reason she was here, to forget what waited for her in Los Angeles. She'd determined to play the role she'd been given and look neither forward nor back. She'd done such a good job of it that she'd almost managed to forget reality completely.

"I wish I'd never seen those damned files."

Drew said nothing. He couldn't bring himself to agree with her. He'd been trying to bring Davis down for too long. But there was a part of him that wished the same thing, that wished it had been someone else who'd brought them the information they needed. Anyone but Kate.

He was not even conscious that he'd moved until he saw his hands close over her shoulders, felt the softness of her through the cotton of her shirt. She was trembling, an almost imperceptible shiver running over her. Drew felt something hard and tight in his chest, something he couldn't—wouldn't—put a name to.

"You're going to be all right," he said, his voice rough with emotion. He turned her to face him. "You're going to be all right." As if repeating it could make it a fact.

Kate smiled, but he could see the shimmer of tears in her eyes. "It's stupid," she muttered, brushing impatiently at the moisture that threatened to overflow. "It's this dumb cold that's making me weepy. I know you'll take care of me."

She gave him a watery smile that seemed to go straight inside him, causing a funny little ache in his chest.

"Don't cry." Her cheek was petal soft beneath his fingers as he brushed away the last traces of dampness. At his touch, Kate's breathing developed an odd little catch to it.

And suddenly there was a new element in the atmosphere, a new tension that edged its way between them. She looked up at him, her eyes all golden green and full of questions.

Full of need.

Drew didn't know how to answer the questions, but he understood the need. The hunger. It was the same hunger that had been gnawing at him for days. Or was it weeks? Maybe it was all his life. It was a hunger he couldn't define. Or maybe he was afraid to define it. But he knew exactly what it would take to satisfy it.

Kate.

"Don't cry," he said again, hardly aware of speaking, hardly aware of drawing her closer.

Ignoring the small voice of reason that told him he was making a mistake, Drew lowered his head, moving slowly, giving her time to pull back. Time to stop the madness before it started.

But Kate didn't want to stop it. She'd been waiting for this, wanting it forever. It didn't matter that she'd only known Drew a few weeks. She'd been waiting all her life for this moment, this man.

His mouth was warm against hers. The first touch was light, undemanding. A gentle kiss, meant to offer nothing but comfort. It could have stopped there, could have ended with only that small touch. If Kate hadn't reached up to set her hands on his chest. If Drew hadn't drawn her just a fraction closer. If hunger long denied hadn't welled up in both of them.

It was impossible to know whether Drew's mouth hardened over hers, demanding a deeper surrender, or whether Kate's lips opened even before his tongue came out to trace the fullness of her lower lip.

There was nothing tentative in the embrace, no sense that they needed to ease into it, to discover each other's wants and needs. There was too much pent-up hunger for that, too many weeks of wanting and not having, of needing and pretending not to.

Kate's fingers curled against his chest, feeling the solid strength of muscle beneath his shirt. Drew's tongue slid into the welcoming cavern of her mouth, tasting the heat of her response as her tongue twined with his.

His fingers found the elastic band that secured her hair and pulled it loose. Her hair tumbled across his hand like pale brown satin and he buried his fingers in it, cupping the back of her skull, tilting her head so that he could deepen the kiss.

Kate felt as if everything in the world had disappeared but the two of them. The fact that they would never have met if her life hadn't been in danger didn't seem relevant. This was right. This was what she'd been longing for all her life.

She rose up on her toes, fitting her body more closely to the lean planes of his, needing to feel him with every inch of her being. Drew murmured something indistinguishable against her mouth and slid one hand the length of her spine, trailing fire in its wake. When his fingers splayed across her bottom, Kate arched her hips forward and heard him groan with approval as the movement brought her firmly against his rapidly hardening arousal.

His fingers left her hair, dropping to her waist before sliding up to rest against the side of her breast. Kate caught her breath, her body tensing in anticipation, in need. And then his palm was closing over her breast, burning through the fabric of bra and shirt.

She gasped, her head falling back against his shoulder as her knees weakened. Drew's mouth left hers, trailing a string of biting kisses the length of her throat before his tongue came out to taste the pulse that beat at the base.

His thumb stroked over her swollen nipple and Kate shuddered, feeling liquid heat pool in the pit of her stomach. When he reached for the buttons of her shirt, she offered no protest. She'd have unbuttoned it herself, but her fingers were shaking too badly.

The rise of passion had been so sudden, the heat so fierce, that they'd been deeply involved before rational thought had a chance to assert itself. Once past that first moment, neither was interested in rational thought, only in slaking a thirst long denied.

If the milk Kate had been warming hadn't reached the boiling point just as Drew's hand was sliding inside Kate's open shirt, there could be little doubt about where the scene would have ended. In Drew's bed. Or Kate's. Or, at the speed they were moving, maybe they wouldn't even have made it that far.

As it was, it took several seconds for the angry hissing of hot milk on the even hotter burner to penetrate. Drew dragged his mouth from the soft temptation of Kate's skin, resting his forehead on hers, his breathing ragged.

"The milk's boiling over," Kate said after a moment when he made no effort to move farther. To tell the truth, she didn't really care if the house was on fire.

But the moment had been broken and reality was already popping up between them. Drew's hand slid away from her and he absently tugged the edges of her shirt back together. Reaching over her shoulder, he twisted the burner off and the milk subsided back into the pan.

Kate stood in front of him, caught between his broad frame and the stove. She knew she should move away, but she more than half hoped that they might take up where they'd left off.

Drew slanted her a quick look from under his lashes, his expression unreadable. His eyes seemed to linger on her mouth, swollen from his kisses, and Kate held her breath, wanting him to take her in his arms, unable to move the few inches that would have put her there.

And then he was stepping back, putting distance between them. And the room seemed suddenly a great deal cooler. Her face still, she brought her hands up and began sliding buttons into buttonholes. She was pleased to see that her fingers were reasonably steady, though she couldn't imagine how it was possible considering her pulse was still racing.

"That shouldn't have happened." Drew's voice was husky. He looked at her, looked away.

"You were trying to comfort me," Kate said, willing to come to his rescue when he couldn't seem to think of anything else to say. "It's all right, Drew. Things just got a little out of hand for a minute."

"That's an understatement." He shook his head, his expression disbelieving, as if he still couldn't quite absorb what had just happened—what had almost happened.

"Well, no harm done," she said, trying to sound brusque. The truth was, if she hadn't been surreptitiously leaning against the counter, she wasn't at all sure that her knees would have supported her.

"No harm done," he repeated, not looking quite as relieved as she might have expected.

No harm done at all unless you counted the fact that she was very much afraid she was falling in love with him.

Chapter Seven

Since sleep proved elusive, Kate had plenty of time to think about what had happened—what had nearly happened—between her and Drew. In the dark hours just before dawn, she decided that it was an obvious case of propinquity. Nothing more profound than that.

Circumstances had thrown the two of them together and forced them to rely on each other. It was only natural that two young, healthy adults should be attracted to each other. Under normal circumstances, they might have crossed paths, been mildly attracted and gone their separate ways without giving it another thought. But circumstances were far from normal, and the time they'd been forced to spend together had simply blown the attraction all out of proportion.

And her bizarre idea that she might be falling in love with him could be chalked up to the same cause. She'd been frightened, abruptly reminded of her own mortality. Drew was, it seemed, all that stood between her and a rude introduction to that mortality. And for a moment, she'd fancied herself in love with him. Sort of a twist on the Stockholm Syndrome where people fell in love with their captors. Now that she understood it, she could watch that it didn't get out of hand.

Propinquity, plain and simple. Nothing to worry about.

Which was exactly what she'd tell Drew when she saw him.

He'd retreated to his den the night before and hadn't come out until nearly midnight. Kate knew exactly when he'd gone to his room because she'd still been awake and had heard his footsteps go down the hall. She'd also heard them pause outside her door and had held her breath, not sure whether to hope that he continued on his way, or pray that he opened the door and came in.

Now that she'd gotten a handle on the problem, she was glad that her door had stayed shut. Very glad, she told herself, refusing to acknowledge even the smallest pang of doubt.

When Drew stepped into the kitchen, it was their first meeting since their shattering embrace the night before. Kate looked up from the crossword puzzle she'd been staring at for the past thirty minutes, though she hadn't yet filled in a single clue. Their eyes crossed briefly and she felt her heart bump. Nerves, she told herself. It had nothing to do with the ice blue of his eyes or the chiseled line of his jaw.

"Good morning," she said, forcing her voice to sound normal.

"Morning." Drew reached for the coffee she'd made, nodding his thanks as he poured his first cup and sipped the steaming brew. He turned to face her, leaning one hip on the counter.

"I've been doing a lot of thinking," he began.

"So have I," Kate interrupted. "And I know exactly what happened last night."

"You do?" Drew raised one brow. He wasn't sure what he'd expected, but he hadn't been anticipating her cheerful smile. She looked as if nothing had happened. Considering the way he felt, he wasn't at all sure he liked seeing her look so calm.

"I do." She smiled and reached for her coffee, and Drew found himself unreasonably pleased to see that her hand was not quite steady. So she wasn't as unmoved as she was trying to appear.

"Then maybe you can explain it to me." For some reason, seeing evidence that she was not as cool as she seemed made him feel better.

"Propinquity."

"What?" Drew's brows nearly disappeared in the thick wave of black hair that lay on his forehead.

"Propinquity," Kate said again, her smile determined. "It was almost inevitable, really."

"It was?"

"Well, yes." She shrugged, but he noticed that she was clinging to her coffee cup as if it were a life preserver.

"So you're not upset?" he probed.

"Of course not. There's nothing to be upset about. It was just that there I was. And there you were..."

"And there we were," he finished dryly when she seemed to run out of words.

"Yes. There we were." The memory of just where they'd been seemed to dry up her well of good humor momentarily. Her eyes dropped from his and she swallowed visibly, the color running up her cheeks. But she grabbed determinedly for the explanation she'd decided on.

"It was bound to happen."

"You think so?" Drew kept his tone carefully neutral.

Not that he didn't agree with her. It had been bound to happen. If there was one thing he'd decided during last night's sleeplessness, it was that. From the moment he'd seen her picture, there'd been something drawing him to her, something more than just the fact that she was a part of his job.

"Well, look at the situation. Here we are, the two of us stuck away from everything and everyone, pretending that we're married." Kate shrugged. "It seems obvious that, sooner or later, something like...last night was bound to happen."

"Probably." Drew noticed that she stumbled over finding a description of what had happened between them. Not that he could have done any better. Wildfire? Conflagration? Detonation?

"Well, now that it's happened, we can forget about it." She didn't seem as relieved by his apparent agreement as he might have expected. Was there just the faintest trace of disappointment in her eyes?

"So you just want to forget it?" he asked.

"It seems best, don't you think?" She got up and went to the sink to rinse her cup. "It happened and we got through it. Now we can forget about it."

"Propinquity?" He sidestepped the issue of forgetting.

"Propinquity," she said firmly. She smiled in his general direction, but Drew noticed that her eyes showed a tendency to sheer away from him.

"Hmm." She seemed to take the noncommittal murmur for agreement and her smile brightened another notch.

"I'm glad we could talk about it. It's always better to get things out in the open. I read once that almost any problem can be resolved if people just talk about it."

"Probably true."

"Yes." She hesitated, as if feeling that something more should be said. Drew offered no help, sipping at his cooling coffee and letting the silence stretch.

"Well, I'm going to go make my bed," she said at last, sounding as if the task might take all day.

"Thanks for the coffee," Drew said, lifting his cup.

"You're welcome." There was another brief pause and then she gave him a quick, meaningless smile and beat a hasty retreat.

Drew watched her go, wondering if he should feel guilty that he hadn't made the conversation any easier for her. He reached for the coffeepot and freshened his cup. He wrapped one hand around the warm porcelain, his eyes focused on nothing at all.

Propinquity? He could think of several words that described it better. Hunger. Lust. Need. Any one of them was a better match than propinquity. Only a woman could have come up with such a word, he thought, shaking his head in disgust. No man would dismiss a near explosion like last night's embrace with a namby-pamby word like propinquity.

Still, maybe she was partially right. Maybe what had happened last night was the result of the two of them being thrown together like this. God knew he couldn't think of another acceptable excuse. Not that there *was* an acceptable excuse.

Forgetting that he'd refilled the cup, Drew took a large swallow of coffee, wincing as it scalded the inside of his mouth. But a scalded tongue was the least of his problems. The biggest problem he had at the moment was coming to terms with his own thoroughly unprofessional behavior.

He frowned down into his coffee, his thoughts circling back over the same ground they'd covered repeatedly during the night. He was an officer of the law, assigned to protect a witness. A witness, moreover, who was testifying on a case he had a personal interest in seeing brought to a successful conclusion.

He was supposed to be protecting Kate, not kissing her. If the milk hadn't boiled over when it had, they wouldn't have stopped at kisses. He should have been grateful for the interruption, but he had to admit that gratitude was not what he felt. What he felt was frustration that things hadn't progressed to their natural conclusion.

And *that* was a very bad sign, indeed.

He downed the last of the coffee, hardly noticing the discomfort as it stung his already burned mouth. He was a cop. A good cop. He set the cup down with a thump. He'd been known to bend a rule or two, but only if it helped the system work the way it was meant to. From the day he'd pinned on his badge, he'd never forgotten who and what he was.

Until he met Kate Sloane.

Somehow, with Kate, it was easy to forget that he was a cop first and a man second. Even now, in the clear light of day, when he should have been consumed with guilt, all he could think about was how it had felt to kiss her, the soft, silky weight of her breast in his hand and the eager response she'd given him.

"Damn." He was getting aroused just thinking about it. "Damn, damn, damn."

He was obviously losing his mind. Last night he'd stepped over the line. If he wasn't careful, he was going to step over it again, and this time he might step so far there'd be no getting back. He was simply going to have to keep his distance.

Right. Like you did before.

The jeering mental comment made him wince. But he couldn't change what had already happened. All he could do was make sure it didn't happen again.

No matter how much he wanted it.

FOR THE NEXT few days, Kate and Drew played a game of "let's pretend." They pretended they'd never kissed. They pretended that the attraction wasn't still simmering between them. And most of all they pretended that the kiss and the conclusion it hadn't reached was not the main thing on both their minds.

It occurred to Kate that if Drew had been looking for a way to distract her from her worries about being found by Davis, he certainly couldn't have chosen a more effective method. The knowledge that her former boss was looking for her, most probably planning to kill her, just didn't seem as real and vivid as those few minutes in Drew's arms.

It was starting to sink in that her life wasn't ever going to be the same. No matter what happened at the trial, she wasn't going to be able to go back to her old life. Not just because of a possible threat from Davis, but because she was simply no longer the same person she had been.

It was a frightening thought, and one she wasn't quite ready to examine too closely, not any more than she could bring herself to look closely at her feelings for Drew Hunter. She wanted to—had to—accept her own explanation that she'd momentarily gotten gratitude confused with love. She could not—would not—fall in love with the man.

IF PROPINQUITY was the source of their problems, then the obvious solution would have been to put some distance between them. Unfortunately circumstances dictated otherwise. They were stuck with each other until word came that it was safe to go back to Los Angeles.

Which left only the option of pretending that nothing had changed when, in reality, everything had changed. It was not a comfortable solution. The house, not particularly large to start with, soon began to seem like little more than a hut.

Where before, it hadn't presented too much of a challenge to avoid each other, now it seemed as if every time Kate turned around, she bumped into

Drew. And every time she bumped into him, she had to remind herself that the fact that her heart beat faster when he was near was just a result of the situation they were in.

It wasn't really Drew Hunter she was attracted to—it was the fact that he was helping to keep her alive. And the fact that he had eyes the pale blue of a winter sky and shoulders that seemed made for pillowing a woman's head and a mouth that... But those were the sorts of things she wasn't going to think about.

KATE SET TWO SQUARES of fabric together and slid the needle into the beginning of the seam. The late news mumbled from the television in the corner, but she didn't pay much attention to it. Any more than she was paying much attention to her sewing. The fact was, with Drew in the room it was difficult to concentrate on anything.

Since the KISS, which Kate had begun to think of in capital letters, the only time they'd spent together had been while watching the news before going to bed. It had occurred to her that, to anyone looking in the window, they must look like exactly what they were pretending to be—a married couple ending the day in front of the television.

Of course, if they were really married, she wouldn't have found Drew's presence so distracting. She might actually have been able to pay attention to what was on the screen rather than noticing—not for the first time—how good he looked in the faded jeans that hugged his legs. Or how well he filled out the black T-shirt that stretched across his chest.

"Damn!" The exclamation was startled from her as the point of the needle jabbed into her skin. She smiled and shook her head as she met Drew's eyes. Lifting the injured finger to her mouth, she licked away the droplet of blood.

DREW WATCHED AS Kate sucked lightly at the small wound. The television was droning in the background, but he no longer had any idea what the newscaster was saying. He couldn't pull his eyes from the sight of Kate's lips pressed against her finger.

His body tightened with the memory of how those lips had felt against his, with the fantasy of how they'd feel against his skin. He'd spent three days trying to pretend that one kiss had never happened. It seemed the memory only grew more vivid.

He dragged his eyes from her and stared unseeingly at the flickering screen. What the hell had happened to his self-control? He had to be losing his mind to be getting aroused just by the sight of a woman's finger in her mouth.

But the worst part of it was that it wasn't just any woman who made him feel this way. If what he'd experienced had been only generic lust, he would have felt nothing more than a vague annoyance with himself. But he didn't want any woman but Kate Sloane, and that scared the hell out of him.

If he stayed in this room another minute, he wasn't sure he could count on his self-control holding. And next time he kissed her, it was going to take something approaching a nuclear blast to remind him of reality.

He glanced at Kate, ready to offer some banal excuse about retiring early. But Kate's attention was riveted to the television, her hands frozen on the quilt block she'd been sewing.

"The body of Joseph Smithson was discovered in a hotel room in downtown San Francisco yesterday afternoon. Police are unwilling to speculate at this time, but they do admit that the execution-style murder could be the work of organized crime."

There was a picture of a man in the upper right corner of the screen. An ordinary-looking man, slightly balding, a little overweight. Nothing particularly heroic looking about him.

"Smithson was a key witness four years ago in the Gambini murder trial, which resulted in the conviction of two members of the Stephani family. Smithson was..."

Drew snapped off the television. But he knew it was too late. As if he could read her mind, he knew what was going through Kate's head. She didn't need to hear the rest of the story. She didn't need to see Joseph Smithson's picture. It was locked in her brain. An ordinary-looking man who'd done the right thing, testified at a trial and helped convict two murderers.

And now, four years later, he was dead.

There was something chilling about the fact that they hadn't killed him right away. Somehow the delay seemed particularly cold, as if they'd simply been letting him live a little while, letting him hope that he wasn't going to pay the price for his testimony. Like a cat playing with a mouse.

Kate's face was pale and set, her eyes haunted. Drew let his fingers drop away from the switch, but he continued to stand there, wishing there was something he could say, some reassurance he could offer. He wanted to go to her, take her in his arms and tell her that he'd keep her safe, that he wasn't going to let anything happen to her.

Instead, he stayed where he was, saying nothing, doing nothing.

After a moment, Kate moved. She slid the needle very carefully into the fabric and then set the partially sewn block on the end table beside her chair, arranging the pieces very carefully. She set her thimble just so beside the block and shifted the box of pins a quarter of an inch to bring it into precise alignment with the thimble.

Drew watched her, trying not to notice the faint trembling of her hands, curling his fingers into his palms against the urge to pull her into his arms and hold her until the trembling went away.

"I'm tired now," she said, her voice flat and without expression. "I think I'll go to bed a little early."

She stood and offered him a quick, meaningless smile, her eyes sliding across his face without meeting his.

"Good night."

"Good night, Kate."

He watched her leave, feeling as if he should have said something, done something, offered her some reassurance. But what could he have said? That she wasn't putting herself at risk? That what happened to Joseph Smithson would never happen to her? She'd know the first for a lie, and the second for a promise he couldn't keep.

"Damn." Drew shoved his fingers through his dark hair, feeling frustration churn in the pit of his stomach.

He didn't like what was happening to him. He didn't like the fact that he couldn't seem to maintain any kind of professional distance on this case. He didn't like the fact that the woman who should have been only a witness he was to protect had become a great deal more. He didn't like finding that the control on which he'd always prided himself was not as impervious as he'd thought.

Most of all, he didn't like the ache in the pit of his stomach when he thought about the end of this assignment, when his responsibility for Kate would end and he'd have to walk away from her.

"Damn. Damn. Damn." Repeating it didn't help. He felt all knotted up inside, angry with everything and nothing. He wanted to slam out of the house and run and run until he was too exhausted to think. He wanted to walk down the hall and push open Kate's door and find her waiting for him, eager for his touch, as hungry for him as he was for her.

Drew closed his eyes, feeling his body respond to the mental image of her, her skin like silk under his hands, her hair spread out on the pillow, her body arching upward, her legs shifting restlessly, her eyes almost pure green with hunger. She'd whisper his name.

"Drew."

For a moment, the sound of his name seemed a part of the fantasy in his mind. It wasn't until she spoke again that he realized Kate's voice wasn't in his head.

"Drew."

He spun to face her, grateful that he was standing out of the lamplight, knowing that his arousal would have been obvious if he hadn't been. He felt like a fool, and there was a quick flare of anger that she could do this to him without even being in the room. But the anger vanished, replaced by a rush of hunger almost powerful enough to bring him to his knees.

She'd already changed for bed and was wearing the virginal white nightgown that had haunted more of his dreams than he was willing to admit. The rounded neckline bared her collarbone before the gown dropped softly to her knees. It looked like something out of a Victorian novel, not the kind of thing to fuel a man's fantasies. And he'd never seen anything more arousing in his life.

Until he saw her eyes.

He felt his mouth go dry at the look in them, at the need that reflected his own. She didn't have to say a word for him to know what she was thinking, what she was feeling.

"Go to bed, Kate." His voice was hardly more than a whisper but she heard him.

"Come with me."

It was a siren's call, the words stroking over him with an almost physical touch. Drew clenched his hands into fists, trying to remember all the reasons he couldn't do what she was asking, what he wanted more than anything.

"You're upset," he managed finally. "You're not thinking clearly."

"I'm thinking clearly for the first time in days." Her voice trembled, but her words didn't falter. "I'm tired of pretending, Drew. I'm tired of pretending I don't want you. That you don't want me."

If she'd had any doubts about the rightness of what she was doing, they'd disappeared the moment she'd seen him. She'd gone to her room to get ready for bed and the newscast had played in her mind on an endless loop, only it hadn't been Joseph Smithson's face they were showing. It had been hers.

It had come to her, more powerfully than ever before, that life was short, and that hers might be even shorter than she might have anticipated. She'd felt fear and then anger and then a quick rush of determination that she was going to live life to its fullest. No matter what happened later, she didn't want to look back with regret for the things she could have done.

Before she could change her mind, she'd left her room, hurrying down the hall, praying that Drew was still up. She wasn't quite sure her courage would extend to tracking him down in his bedroom. But she was in luck—or not, depending on how you looked at it. Drew was standing where she'd left him, one hand resting on top of the television.

She saw him stiffen when she spoke his name, read the wariness in his eyes when he turned to look at her. And she felt rather than saw the hunger in him. It was that hunger that gave her the courage to step into the room, to walk toward him.

"Go to bed, Kate." There was a ragged edge of desperation in the repeated command. She ignored the words, listening instead to the ache in his voice.

"Come with me," she said again. She stopped in front of him. Later she'd wonder at her own boldness. Later she'd be shocked at her actions. But here and now, all she could think of was that it shouldn't have taken so long to reach this point.

Drew stared down at her, telling himself that he was going to walk away, that this wasn't going to go any further. He drew in a deep breath, his head filling with the scent of her, soap and shampoo. He saw his hands come up to settle on her shoulders. To push her away, he told himself.

"This is wrong." He wasn't sure whether he was asking her or telling her.

"It feels right." She leaned into his touch and he let his elbows bend, let her weight carry her closer.

"I'm supposed to be protecting you."

"Then you shouldn't let me out of your sight." Her hands came up to rest against his chest and Drew felt their touch burn through the fabric of his T-shirt.

He lowered his head, brushing his mouth over her forehead. This couldn't go any further. He had to stop this now before it got out of hand, as if it wasn't already out of hand.

"This has to stop."

"Why?" She turned her face up to his, her mouth a whisper away.

"It's just not right." His eyes searched hers, seeing his own need reflected there.

"You want me."

As if to prove her point, Kate let one hand slide down his chest. Drew sucked in a harsh breath as her fingers slipped past his belt and settled on the hard bulge of his arousal.

"Kate." Her name was a protest. A plea. Aching need and weakening resistance.

One hand left her shoulder. He'd intended to draw her hand away, to set her from him, to walk—no run—from temptation. But somehow his fingers were cupping one of her breasts, feeling the sweet weight of it through the thin white cotton of her nightgown.

She drew in a quick breath and he watched as the color came up in her cheeks, a soft flush of pleasure. Without his volition, his thumb brushed over her taut nipple, his eyes on her face. He saw the flush deepen, saw her mouth part to allow her to draw a shaken breath.

And he was lost.

With a groan, he lowered his head, giving in to the hunger that boiled in him, the need that had been gnawing at his gut for weeks. Kate's mouth opened to his, her eager response fanning the heat building in him.

There was nothing tentative about their coming together. This might have been only the second kiss they'd shared and yet each seemed to know just what the other needed.

Drew shifted his hands on her, flattening one against her back, letting the other sweep down to cup her buttocks, crushing her up against him. Kate whimpered against his mouth, her legs instinctively shifting apart to cradle the hardness of his arousal against her feminine core.

Drew groaned and rocked his hips forward, torturing himself with the feel of her, so close and yet still out of reach. His mouth opened over hers, his tongue plunging deep to find and tangle with hers. God, she tasted like heaven. Her response was everything he'd dreamed, everything he'd remembered from that all-too-brief encounter in the kitchen.

Afterward, neither of them could have said just how they reached Drew's bedroom. It didn't matter. Nothing mattered beyond this long overdue coming together. Oddly enough, once in the dim intimacy of his room, Kate's earlier confidence seemed to disappear. The fingers that had so boldly cupped him a few moments ago now fumbled with the buckle of his belt. And when Drew's hands found their way beneath the hem of her nightgown, Kate's fingers could only cling to his belt as her knees began to tremble.

His hands stroked upward along her thighs, pausing to cup the rounded softness of her bottom. His mouth caught hers in a long, drugging kiss. His hands urged her forward until she felt the hard length of his arousal pressed to the supple skin of her stomach through the denim of his jeans. She shifted instinctively, wanting to get closer, needing to feel him against her. Drew groaned, rocking his hips forward, his tongue thrusting into her mouth in an unmistakable rhythm.

Kate whimpered, her head falling back, her surrender complete. She'd never have believed she could feel so completely, deliciously wanton. The past, the future—both were unimportant. All that mattered was this man and the fact that she'd waited all her life for him—for this moment.

Drew's hands swept upward, taking the soft cotton nightgown with them. Kate lifted her arms and the gown drifted from her, settling to the floor in a white pool. She felt a moment's shy uncertainty at standing in front of him completely nude. She had a woman's instant awareness of the ten extra pounds she'd never quite managed to lose. Her hands shifted, half lifting as if to cover herself, but the movement was never completed.

"My God, you're beautiful." Drew's voice was husky.

"No, I'm not." The protest was automatic.

"Yes, you are." His fingers against her mouth stilled her denial. "I've never in my life wanted anything the way I want you."

His eyes never left her as his fingers trailed down her throat, pausing to test the pulse that beat so frantically at its base. Kate felt as if his touch was stealing her voice, draining away every thought, leaving her capable only of feeling.

"Unbutton my shirt," he whispered, still holding her with that clear blue look.

Fingers trembling, she lifted her hands to his chest, sliding buttons through impossibly small buttonholes. She'd nearly completed the task when his hands drifted downward to cup her breasts. Kate gasped at the feel of him touching her.

How many nights had she lain awake imagining—trying not to imagine—what it would feel like to have him touch her? Her imagination had fallen far short of reality. He caught her nipples between thumb and forefinger of each hand, plucking gently. Kate's head fell back, her fingers clinging to the edges of his open shirt. She felt the touch at her breasts, felt it deeper still in the heavy, damp heat that pooled in the most private part of her.

When he bent his head and his mouth closed over one swollen nipple, she moaned low in her throat, hardly recognizing the sound as hers. Her fingers came up to clasp his head as his teeth abraded the tender bud before his tongue soothed the puckered flesh.

Kate's knees gave out completely. If it hadn't been for Drew's support, she would have sunk to the floor. His mouth lifted, catching hers again as he turned, lowering her onto the bed. Kate felt the bed dip beneath her weight and then felt him moving away. She reached up blindly, feeling something close to panic at the thought that he was leaving her, that she might not find the end of the journey they'd begun.

Drew's hands were shaking so badly, he had trouble unbuckling his belt. Seeing Kate lying beneath him, her slender body flushed with desire, her eyes almost pure green with need, he felt an almost savage hunger sweep over him. *This* was what he'd wanted from the moment he'd first seen her picture. He'd never felt this gut-level response to a woman before, never felt so close to the edge of control.

He finally wrenched open the belt, feeling as if he might explode if he didn't free himself, if he couldn't sheathe himself in her, feel the silken heat of her close around him. He reached for the zipper tab, but Kate's fingers were there first.

"Let me."

Drew's hands fell to his sides, his fingers curling into his palms as she inched the zipper down. It seemed to take forever. He could feel the backs of her fingers rubbing against his swollen flesh, a sweet torture through the denim of his jeans. She seemed to be having trouble with the task, her hand lingering until he was sure he would burst. And then he caught her eyes, saw the wicked gleam in them and realized she was deliberately lingering over it, enjoying the power she had over him.

"Witch." The word was a thick accusation as he caught her hand in his, crushing it to him for an instant before he quickly finished the job. He stripped off his jeans and shorts in one quick motion and set one knee on the edge of the bed, looming over her like a conquering warrior.

And then she opened her arms to him, her hips lifting in sweet invitation and he knew he was the one being conquered. The very force of his need made him hesitate for a moment. This was such madness. It was against all the rules.

"Drew." His name was a breath, a sigh. And he was lost.

"God, Kate."

He came to her in a rush, his hips sliding between her thighs, his hardness finding her softness. As in their kiss, there was no need for tentative exploration, for hesitation. He sheathed himself in her with one long, smooth thrust.

She cried out, her neck arching as she pressed her head back into the pillow, and she welcomed him into her. He felt that welcome in the way her hands clung to his hips, drawing him closer as her knees drew up on either side of his body, cradling him as she took him deep into herself.

It was completion. An emptiness filled. An emptiness that was only partly physical. Kate knew that in her entire life she'd never been whole. Not until this moment. Not until this man.

He shifted, withdrawing from her and then thrusting home again. She moaned low in her throat, her eyes tightly closed as he repeated the movement, each new thrust seeming to take him deeper than the last, each making him even more a part of her.

The world narrowed to that one room, to the bed on which they lay and finally to the sweet friction of his body on hers, within hers. Kate felt tension building in the pit of her stomach, like a spring being coiled tighter and tighter until the sensation became almost painful.

Her head twisted against the covers they'd been in too much of a hurry to pull down. She'd never known anything could feel so intense. She wanted him to stop, knew she'd surely fly apart if he didn't stop. And yet her hands clung to him, feeling the dampness of sweat on his back, feeling the tautness of his muscles as he fought to hold his own completion back long enough to allow her to reach hers.

And then she did fly apart, spinning outward into a million pieces as her body arched against his, her eyes jerking open to stare up into his face in astonished wonder as the tension exploded into fulfillment.

Drew held back, watching the color run up from her breasts to her face, seeing her eyes go wide and startled and then seeing them grow heavy with pleasure. Only then did he let himself go, letting the soft contractions of her pleasure take him over the edge into his own satisfaction.

Kate felt the first shudder run through him, felt him swell inside her, saw his face go taut as his climax took him. Instinctively she arched her hips, taking him still deeper, letting her muscles contract around him. She felt him shudder in her arms, felt him throb inside her and knew that she'd never in her life felt complete.

Knew, too, that she'd never again feel complete except with this man. All her determination had failed. It wasn't propinquity at all.

It was love.

And God help her.

Chapter Eight

Drew felt as if he'd been drugged. Every muscle and bone felt heavy, relaxed in a way he'd never known. Even when he'd been in the hospital and they'd been pumping him full of pain medication, he hadn't felt so completely relaxed. Of course, then he'd been fighting the drugs, determined to recover without their help, resenting that he needed them, even for a short while.

He was through fighting his need for Kate Sloane. Through pretending it didn't exist. He didn't know why, didn't understand what it was between them, but for the moment, at least, he couldn't pretend anymore.

He'd just sent every rule of ethics up in flames, set himself up for dismissal—a dismissal he couldn't even argue he didn't deserve. The argument could be made that he'd compromised a witness, maybe even jeopardized a case that meant a lot to him, personally and professionally.

And the only thought in his head was to wonder how soon he could do it again.

It took every ounce of strength he could muster to lift himself off Kate's warm body and roll onto the bed. Even then, he swept one arm beneath her, pulling her up against his side. Without looking at it too closely, he knew he wanted her as close as it was possible to be without the two of them being physically joined. If it hadn't been for the fact that he was too heavy for her, he wouldn't have left her at all.

If he'd thought that making love to her would quench the hunger that had been gnawing at him for weeks, he knew already that he'd been dead wrong. His body felt heavy—sated. Yet he could already feel hunger stirring deep inside—a need he couldn't quite define and was afraid to examine too closely. The thought made him stir uneasily.

His arm tightened around Kate as she settled against him, pillowing her head on his shoulder and throwing one leg across his hips. She curled up to him as if it were the most natural thing in the world. As if they really were what they were pretending to be—husband and wife.

"This isn't real."

Though his voice was low and husky, the abrupt words sounded loud in the quiet room. He felt Kate stiffen slightly, her body tensing as if in defense against a potential blow.

"This isn't real," he said again, wondering just who he was trying to remind—Kate or himself.

"It feels real," Kate said, her tone deliberately light. Her hand stroked over his chest, her fingers threading through the mat of black hair that covered his muscles.

"But it's not. This is all just pretend."

She flinched as if the words had a physical impact. Drew cursed under his breath, wishing he could call them back and yet knowing they had to be said. One of them had to retain some grasp of reality, no matter how fragile that hold was.

"Kate..."

"Don't." She lifted her head from his shoulder and braced herself on her elbow so that she could look down at him. "Let's pretend."

"But..."

"Please, Drew." She set the tips of her fingers against his mouth, silencing him. "Just for a little while. What can it hurt?"

They both knew it could end up hurting a great deal. They weren't children, playing at house. They were adults, already playing a dangerous game. Adding a new element of pretend could be fatal, in more ways than one.

Drew reached up to stroke her tangled hair back from her face, knowing he should force her—force both of them—to look at what they'd done in a cold, hard light. But in her eyes, he saw traces of the fear that had driven her to him, the fear that her life might be over before it had really begun. And he saw a need that echoed his own, the same hunger he'd felt for weeks.

"God, I must be crazy."

Kate's smile was his reward. He slid his fingers deeper into her hair, drawing her face down to his, catching her mouth in a slow, drugging kiss. Kate didn't argue, either with his statement or with the kiss.

IT WAS, DREW FOUND, frighteningly easy to pretend. Easier than it had been when he was a child. Growing up in foster homes had left him with a cold appreciation for the truth. At first, he'd tried to convince himself that he was truly wanted by the families that took him in, not just for the extra money his presence brought them or even out of a genuine concern for those less fortunate, but that they really wanted *him*.

By the time he was eight he'd realized that there was no sense in pretending he was a part of any of the families he stayed with. No matter how nice they were, he was still an outsider, never really a part of the inner circle. He'd been lucky in some ways. He'd never been abused, always been clothed and fed. It hadn't been a physical hunger he'd felt but an emotional one. The human need to matter to someone, to love and be loved.

Long before he grew to adulthood, he'd learned to close off the part of him that craved affection.

There had been no sense in pretending to be anything other than what he was—a boarder, occasionally unwelcome. To pretend that he might really become a part of the family was to guarantee nothing but hurt when it came time to move again.

His marriage to Diane had proven, once and for all, that he was incapable of making the sort of emotional connections that were necessary to sustain a relationship. He'd accepted that with no real regrets. And if he'd occasionally felt an ache that might have been loneliness, he'd shrugged it off. He was what he was and nothing was going to change that.

So how was it that Kate Sloane had managed to make him doubt what he was? Made him think about things he'd put out of his life a long time ago—things like home and family?

When he was with her, it was easy to forget reality, forget the future.

And it was remarkably easy to pretend that they weren't living in a dream world.

"I THINK THE HOUSE would look better green." Kate frowned at the house, narrowing her eyes against the sunlight as if trying to picture the small house painted a different color.

Drew turned his head slowly, reluctant to disturb the pleasant lethargy that had taken hold of him. It had been Kate's idea to bring their take-out chicken dinner into the backyard and have a picnic. He couldn't remember the last time he'd been on a picnic. There must have been occasions when he was a child, but none came to mind.

Though he'd grumbled about the discomforts of sitting on the ground and said that it was ridiculous to eat in the backyard, only yards from a comfortable table where they wouldn't have to worry about ants, Drew had to admit that lying on a blanket spread on the soft green grass and looking up into the spreading branches of the big sycamore tree was not a bad way to spend an afternoon. He'd been on the verge of falling asleep until Kate had made her comment about the house.

"Houses should be white," he said after a moment.

"Houses should be all different colors," she disagreed. "Think how dull a neighborhood would look if every single house was white." She was spinning a dandelion between her fingers, the soft yellow flower almost matching the sleeveless top she wore with her white shorts.

"Organized," Drew corrected, turning his face back up to the dappled sunlight. "It would look organized. You wouldn't have disasters like that purple monstrosity down the street."

That silenced her momentarily. Half a block away was a house that had been painted what could only be described as brothel purple, with eye-searingly white trim. The owners had completed the picture by planting the flower beds in front with orange and red cosmos fronted by marigolds. The combination was arresting, to put it mildly.

"I didn't have in mind anything quite that... cheerful," she said after a moment.

"Cheerful?" Drew raised his brows without bothering to open his eyes. "If that color were any more 'cheerful,' it would be fatal."

Kate grinned but refused to be dissuaded from the topic at hand. "A nice pale green would be perfect, maybe with white trim."

"Houses should be white," Drew repeated. He didn't really care what color the house was, this one or any other. But there was something pleasant about the lazy argument.

"A house should reflect the inherent uniqueness of its occupants." Kate's voice took on the solemnity of a social critic. "Many of today's problems would be solved if people developed a deeper appreciation for the individuality of their neighbors."

"Many of today's problems would be solved if people didn't paint their houses purple."

"Maybe they felt the color deep in their souls." Drew felt her move and caught the faint scent of her shampoo, telling him that she'd shifted closer. Desire stirred in him, the way it always did when she was near. If he'd ever thought that once he'd had Kate the hunger would be slaked, this past week had shown him how wrong he'd been. The more he had of her, the more he wanted.

"The rest of the world feels it in their stomachs. No one could see that house without getting bilious."

"You just don't appreciate the artistic statement they've made."

From the sound of her voice, he guessed that she was lying on her stomach, propped on her elbows beside him. The still, warm air carried her scent—soap and shampoo, fresh, innocent smells. How was it that he'd never noticed how incredibly sensual those scents could be until he'd met Kate Sloane?

"If that house is an artistic statement, I'd hate to meet the artist." It was a nonsensical argument, one neither of them had any interest in winning. It was simply a way to pass a hot, summer afternoon.

He felt Kate shift again, but didn't bother to open his eyes to verify her new position. Then he felt her fingers on the buttons of his shirt. He felt the muscles in his stomach clench in anticipation as she slid first one button loose and then another.

She was a passionate and eager lover, but she didn't often initiate sex, unless he could count the fact that her presence alone was enough to keep him in a state of latent arousal. Kate slipped her hand inside his opened shirt and Drew knew she must be able to feel the accelerated beat of his heart.

For a moment, he felt a flash of anger. Anger at himself for having so little control, anger at Kate for showing him just how fragile that control was.

But the anger was quickly drowned out by the rising tide of hunger and the need that never failed to surprise him. Not since he was a child had he allowed himself to need anyone.

"You're too stuck in the mud," she said softly. Her fingers combed through the soft black hair that covered his chest, and Drew's jeans were suddenly too tight. "What you need is something to shake you up."

"I can think of several things I need more," he told her huskily. He opened his eyes, one hand coming up to catch her arm. But the movement was never completed. He caught a glimpse of Kate's eyes, bright with mischief, and then the remains of a glass of ice water hit him full in the chest.

"What the...?" The words were cut off by the shock of icy water against hot skin. Drew gasped as if the water had hit him full in the face.

"Complacency is bad for you," Kate said, scrambling backward as she rose to her feet.

"So is being strangled." Drew stood, wiping one hand over his chest and then staring at it, hardly able to believe it was really wet.

"Now, Drew, I was just trying to give you a little surprise. Everyone likes surprises."

"You damn near drowned me, you little witch." He advanced toward her.

"It's so hot, I thought you'd enjoy a little cool water."

Drew didn't bother to respond but only continued to move toward her at a slow, deliberate pace that made her heart beat faster. She giggled and backed away.

"I was just trying to be helpful, Drew."

"If I were you, I'd quit while I was ahead," he suggested, his voice soft and menacing.

Kate glanced over her shoulder at the back door, gauging her chances of reaching it before he could catch her. Remembering his lightning-fast reflexes, she wouldn't have placed a bet on herself.

She looked back at Drew, feeling a delicious shiver of fear at the expression on his face. He looked like a jungle cat eyeing a particularly juicy bit of prey. She gave him an ingratiating smile and edged a little closer to the door.

"I read in a magazine once that a good sense of humor is a mark of a well-rounded individual."

"Revenge is one of the strongest human needs," he commented softly.

"Forgiveness is another great quality."

"No crime should go unpunished."

"Now, Drew..." She held out one hand, her nervous protest only half-feigned. She knew he'd never hurt her, but she had to admit to being just a little uncertain of his temper. Maybe the impulse to douse him with ice water had not been one of her better ideas.

"Now, Kate..." His voice was husky, his expression unreadable.

He took a quick step toward her and she shrieked. She still held the plastic cup that had held the water and she flung it at him. It bounced off his chest to land in the grass, but she didn't wait to see it fall. Spinning on her heel, Kate sprinted for the back door, flinging it open and dashing inside.

Drew caught her just inside the door. She had no doubt that he could have caught her sooner. He'd simply allowed her to prolong the chase. Kate's heart was pounding against her breastbone as his weight pinned her back against the wall.

His eyes gleamed down at her—ice blue and yet full of fire. She felt like a maiden caught in the arms of a ruthless pirate, knowing ravishment was only a heartbeat away and yet knowing it would be a sweet ravishment.

"Apologize," he whispered. He pressed closer, his chest dampening her T-shirt.

"I'm sorry you're such a stick-in-the-mud," she offered, finding it difficult to form a coherent sentence. Not that Drew was interested in her apology. She could feel him pressed against her lower stomach, already hard.

"You're asking for trouble." He tilted his head to let his mouth find the soft shell of her ear. Kate felt a shiver run through her as his teeth closed over her earlobe and nibbled gently.

"Did I find it?" She pushed his shirt the rest of the way off his shoulders before letting her fingers settle on his damp chest.

"In spades, sweetheart. In spades."

Her arms clung to his neck as he swept her off her feet and into his arms, carrying her through the kitchen and into the hallway that led to the bedrooms. He shouldered open the door to his room—their room for the past week—and let her slide to her feet beside the bed.

Looking up at him, Kate decided that if this was trouble, she never wanted to be without it again.

THERE WAS A PART of Kate that had recognized from the beginning the fact that she and Drew would be lovers. A deep feminine knowledge that made their coming together inevitable. So inevitable that she felt little surprise when it happened.

What did surprise her was discovering the depths of her own sexuality. Her experience with sex had generally led her to feel that sex was either highly overrated or simply not something for which she had much talent. With Drew, she discovered how completely wrong she'd been. If it hadn't been so clichéd, she'd have been inclined to think that the earth moved when he made love to her.

The other thing that surprised her was the playful side Drew revealed. Once they'd become lovers, some of the mask disappeared, revealing a man who smiled more easily and laughed more often than she'd expected. And every smile, every laugh, served to work his image deeper into her heart.

It was no longer possible for Kate to pretend she didn't love him. Her imagination didn't stretch that far. Oh, she'd tried telling herself that what she felt was sexual fascination, that a lover like Drew made it easy to confuse love with lust.

That might have explained her eagerness to share his bed, but it couldn't explain the warm, melting feeling that came over her every time she looked at him. Nor did it explain away the sharp ache in her chest whenever she let herself remember that the game they were playing had to end soon.

She'd never been good at lying to herself and she didn't try now. She'd fallen in love with Drew Hunter and that was all there was to it. It might be one of the most foolish things she'd ever done, but she didn't compound her foolishness by thinking that Drew had to return her feelings. Despite the new closeness they shared, she couldn't judge his feelings for her. Becoming his lover hadn't made it any easier for her to read his thoughts.

That he desired her was obvious. That a part of him resented that desire was equally obvious. Beyond that, she wasn't sure of anything when it came to Drew Hunter. He was her protector, her lover... and still more than half a stranger. It didn't matter. She loved him. And whatever might await them in the real world, for this little space of time, he was hers and she was going to enjoy every moment of it.

She had the sense of time running out and she was determined to enjoy whatever time remained to them. No matter what happened later, she was going to have these few days or weeks to remember.

DEFT STROKES of the chef's knife cut the carrots into neat diagonal slices. Except for the soft thwack of the knife against the wooden cutting board, the kitchen was quiet. Drew whistled tunelessly under his breath, aware that he couldn't remember the last time he'd felt the sort of deep contentment he felt in that moment.

Kate was taking a shower, the low hum of water running through the old pipes clearly audible in the kitchen. He didn't have to close his eyes to picture her—silky brown hair caught up on top of her head, her wet skin flushed from the heat of the water.

"Damn." The soft exclamation was startled from him as the knife came down uncomfortably close to his thumb. Using the flat of the blade to lift the sliced carrots onto a plate ready for stir-frying later, Drew forced Kate's image from his mind.

He was tempted to join her, but the one time they'd showered together, they'd both nearly ended up with concussions. Wet ceramic tile was a slippery and unforgiving surface. They'd barely made it out of the bathroom and they hadn't made it all the way to the bed. He'd had rug burns on his knees for two days.

He grinned as he reached for a stalk of celery. It had been worth it. More than worth it.

Drawing a deep breath, he sent the knife through the celery with quick, chopping motions. Cooking was his only domestic skill, developed more in self-defense than anything else. Other than the brief years of his marriage, he'd had the choice of learning to cook or of relying on TV dinners and restaurants.

It had turned out to be a handy talent. Kate had a number of domestic talents but cooking was not among them. She cheerfully admitted to being a whiz with a microwave. Beyond that, it was safer not to turn her loose in a kitchen.

Domesticity suits you, Hunter. The half-mocking words made Drew's fingers hesitate over a pile of mushrooms. He hadn't given much thought to Dave Murphy's visit lately, had given even less thought to the reason for it. These past few days had been like stolen time.

It had to come to an end. It couldn't be long now before Lavery called them back to L.A. But he wasn't going to think about that now. He had pretended this long. He could keep reality at bay a little while longer. His mouth curved in a rueful smile. One thing he'd found was that pretending got easier with practice.

With the plate of vegetables neatly sliced, ready to stir-fry with the chicken that was already marinating, Drew turned from the counter and started to clear the table. Kate had set her purse on it when they'd come back from the market earlier and he picked it up, along with two magazines and a paperback novel.

He started to carry the items into the living room, but the snap on Kate's purse was apparently not quite closed and he'd gone only a few feet when its contents started to shower out at his feet. Cursing, he twisted his wrist to bring it upright. But not before he heard something hit the floor with a very solid sound.

Glancing down, Drew froze for an instant. Moving slowly, he sank to his haunches, his left hand coming out. He brushed aside a checkbook, a package of gum, a packet of tissues and half a dozen hairpins. His fingers closed around the solid weight of a .32 automatic.

Dropping the magazines and the book, he checked the clip, finding it fully loaded. The safety was on, but that didn't do anything to ease the sudden grimness around his mouth. Just how long had Kate been carrying a gun?

KATE WAS HUMMING under her breath as she left the bedroom. Her hair was still damp, but it would dry soon enough in the warm evening air. Just before she'd gone in to take a shower, she'd heard Drew whistling in the kitchen, a tuneless sound that expressed the same contentment she felt.

Though she knew little of Drew's past, she didn't need his life history to realize that contentment was something of which he'd known very little. The thought that he'd found it in this little house with her was almost as good as hearing him say that he loved her. Since she didn't dare let herself hope for that, she savored what she did have.

She didn't hear him whistling now, but he was probably in the midst of stirring together whatever he was making for dinner. She stepped into the kitchen, expecting to find Drew standing in front of the stove.

But he wasn't at the stove and there were no savory smells to indicate that dinner was nearly done. Instead, he was standing next to the table, watching her with the same cool eyes she remembered from when they'd first met—the eyes of the cop, not the lover.

"You want to explain this?" Drew's voice matched the ice in his eyes. Kate looked from his face to the gun that lay on his palm to her purse, which sat open on the kitchen table.

"I don't recall giving you permission to go through my purse." She reached for the gun, but he closed his fingers over it, drawing it back out of her reach.

"Your purse was open and the gun fell out when I went to move it." There was nothing apologetic about his explanation. "The question is, what was it doing there in the first place?"

"It's mine." Kate wasn't sure what he'd wanted her to say, but the simple statement obviously wasn't it.

"I figured that out on my own," he said, his tone chilly and sarcastic.

When she didn't respond, Drew's jaw tightened momentarily before relaxing as if with a conscious effort. He set the gun on the table. Out of her reach, Kate noted, wondering if that had been deliberate.

"Have you been carrying this all along?"

"Yes." She lifted her chin and met his eyes. She hadn't done anything wrong and she was darned if she was going to feel guilty. That he was upset was obvious. The reasons weren't so obvious.

"When did you get it?"

"Two years ago. Shouldn't I have an attorney present when I'm being interrogated?" She arched her brows, coolly questioning.

"I'm not interrogating you," he snapped.

"Funny. It *feels* like you are."

"Dammit, Kate!" He stopped and drew a deep breath, releasing it slowly. When he continued, his voice was even. "Did it occur to you to tell me that you were carrying a gun?"

"At first." She shrugged in answer to the question in his eyes. "I didn't know you. I didn't feel obligated to tell you everything."

"What about now? Now that you *know* me, in every sense of the word?"

Kate flushed. She lifted her chin another notch, her eyes cool. "To tell the truth, I more or less forgot about it."

There was a moment of silence while Drew absorbed her words. "You *forgot* you were carrying a gun?"

"No. I forgot to tell you about it."

"You didn't think I'd be interested?" he suggested politely.

"I thought you'd make a production out of it," she corrected. "Obviously I was right."

"I'm not making a production out of it." He stopped and ran the fingers of one hand through his hair, trying to keep hold of his temper.

"I don't suppose I should even bother to ask whether or not you have a license to carry a concealed weapon."

"You know I don't. I don't usually carry it with me. I keep it in the drawer in my nightstand at home."

"But you've been carrying it since we met and you didn't bother to tell me. What are you doing with it in the first place?"

"I bought it a couple of years ago. Someone broke into a house a few blocks away from my apartment. The woman who lived there was raped. It seemed like a good idea for me to have some protection."

"Do you know how to use it?"

"I took a few lessons when I first got it." Kate lifted one shoulder in a half shrug, wishing, not for the first time, that she could read his thoughts.

When she'd entered the room and he'd thrust the gun at her, it had been simple enough. There'd been no mistaking the anger in those glacial blue eyes. But he'd gotten that under control almost immediately and now it was impossible to read anything behind that expressionless mask.

"Were you any good?"

"I hit the center of the target a couple of times," she admitted.

"Great. Now all we need is a law that requires bad guys to have a target painted on their chests. Then you'd be in great shape."

"I don't expect anybody to have a target on their chest," she said stiffly.

"There's a big difference between shooting holes in a paper target and shooting holes in a human being, Kate."

"I know that."

"Do you?" He ran his fingers through his hair again, suddenly more weary than angry. "Do you have any idea what it feels like to shoot someone?"

"Of course not. I've never shot anyone. And I don't have any plans to shoot anyone."

"Then what the hell are you doing with a gun?"

"Any criminal in his right mind is going to run when he sees the way my finger is shaking on the trigger.'' She tried a tentative smile, wanting to coax him out of his bleak mood.

"When you pick up a gun, you'd better be prepared to use it.''

"If the time comes, I'll do what I have to do.''

"Will you?'' he asked, watching her with a brooding expression.

"If I didn't believe I could use it, I wouldn't have bought it.''

He continued to watch her for a moment longer, those ice blue eyes expressionless. Kate met his look, wondering what he was thinking.

"Why are you upset?'' she asked abruptly. "I would have thought you'd approve of my having a little extra protection.''

A good question, Drew thought. Too bad he didn't know the answer. Or didn't want to admit it. He turned away from her and picked up the gun, weighing it in his hand, trying to think of words that would answer her question without revealing things he wasn't sure of himself.

"You don't need extra protection,'' he said finally. "That's my job.''

"You don't think that I have that gun because I think you can't protect me, do you?'' The distress in her voice was mirrored in her eyes. She closed the distance between them and put her hand on his arm. "Drew, I know nothing will happen to me while you're with me.''

He said nothing. Let her think that it was wounded pride that had put the ice in his voice, in his eyes. It was a perfectly reasonable explanation. It was certainly more reasonable than the truth, which was that he'd been angry because the gun had been a reminder that she was in danger, that the past couple of weeks had been a charade.

They'd been playing at happily-ever-after and he'd gotten so involved in the game that he'd almost managed to forget that it *was* a game.

He brought his hand up, his fingers skimming over her cheek. Kate's eyes searched his, asking questions he couldn't—wouldn't—answer. He couldn't tell her that he'd have given almost anything to be able to say that she had nothing to be afraid of, that the danger was a thing of the past.

"Just try not to shoot me," he said at last, his mouth quirking in a half smile.

"I'll try to keep that in mind," Kate promised, wishing for the thousandth time that she could read what he was thinking.

She closed her eyes as he lowered his mouth to hers. Though there was passion in the kiss, there was also a sense of urgency, a feeling that time was slipping away from them. The gun had served as a reminder that their time was finite and that its end was in the near future.

Dinner was forgotten. The gun was forgotten. Nothing mattered but the hunger they felt for each other. The past was unimportant. The future was uncertain. All they had was the present. It was enough. It had to be.

Chapter Nine

Neither of them mentioned the gun again. Drew watched Kate put it back into her purse, his expression deliberately blank. Kate wished she could read his thoughts. Did he think she didn't trust him to protect her? She'd trusted him with her life from the very beginning. It was her heart she was worried about.

But if she told him that, then he'd know that she'd fallen in love with him, and she wasn't quite ready for that. She wasn't sure she'd *ever* be ready. There were moments when she thought he must know how she felt. How could he *not* know? It had to be in her eyes when she looked at him. And every time they made love...surely he could feel it in her touch.

But if he'd guessed how she felt, Kate could never read it in his face. And as far as trying to guess what he felt about her... She'd have had better luck reading the expression on the great Sphinx.

Under ordinary circumstances, she might have made demands, insisted on defining their relationship, asked him to tell her how he felt. But the circumstances were far from ordinary. If they had been, she would probably never have met Drew Hunter. Never have fallen in love with him. Never have wanted so desperately to believe that he loved her.

And never have had to wonder whether or not she'd live long enough to feel the hurt if he *didn't* love her.

"JUST A LITTLE to the left. Now back a few inches. Up a little. There! Hold it and I'll push a little dirt underneath the root ball." Kate's voice bubbled with enthusiasm.

It was an enthusiasm Drew didn't particularly share. But then it was hard to be enthused when he was straddling a hole in the ground, supporting what felt like a thousand pounds of dirt and tree, and trying to hold the whole thing in the position Kate had decreed as correct.

Peering through the mass of leafy branches that were beating him in the face, Drew watched as Kate knelt on the ground and shoved dirt into the hole she'd dug the day before. She was wearing a pair of bright pink shorts and a lime green T-shirt—a traffic-stopping color combination. Her soft brown hair was caught up in a ponytail and decorated with a pink scrunchy thing.

She looked fresh and innocent and full of life, and Drew wanted nothing so much as to drop the stupid tree into the hole, tumble Kate to the soft green grass and make love to her under the fading afternoon sunlight. But then, when didn't he want to make love to her?

"Could you tilt the trunk a little to the right?"

Drew tilted obediently and tried not to think about tugging that bright T-shirt over Kate's head, seeing her eyes go all soft, smoky green and her mouth soften in anticipation of his kiss.

"Hang on just a few more seconds. I just want to make sure there's plenty of dirt underneath so it doesn't sink too low when we set it in." Kate was kneeling on the ground, using her hands to push dirt under the root ball.

As far as Drew was concerned, the tree could sink all the way to the top leaf and he wouldn't object. But Kate was determined that another tree was just what the backyard needed and he'd agreed to help her. He wondered what Lavery would say if he could see him now. Would he comment, the way Murphy had, that domesticity seemed to suit him?

Drew frowned at the slender trunk he was holding. He'd certainly never thought of himself as a domestic animal. His marriage to Diane had seemed to confirm that he was a loner, unsuited to sharing his life with someone. When they'd divorced, he'd felt nothing more than annoyance that he'd made such a monumental mistake and regret that someone else had been hurt by that mistake. He was a loner, and the sooner he accepted it the better. And if, occasionally, loneliness seemed to catch him by the throat, well, better that than trying to be something he wasn't.

Then he was assigned to protect Kate Sloane. In the weeks since they'd met he'd begun to lose sight of just what he was. He was a loner, yet he'd never known contentment until these past few weeks— sharing a house with Kate, feeling it become a home, something he'd never had and never expected to have. He was a cop, but he'd done things no cop had any business doing. And what was worse, he didn't even regret what he'd done.

There were moments when he felt as if he didn't know himself anymore. What the hell had happened to him?

"There. You can set it down now."

Drew was grateful for the interruption. He wasn't sure he liked the direction his thoughts had been taking, a direction they took all too often lately.

He allowed the tree to settle into the hole and then knelt down and began shoving dirt in around the root ball. Kate worked from the opposite side, frowning slightly with concentration as she pushed the soil into place. Drew found himself wanting to lean over and kiss her.

There was hardly a time when he didn't want to kiss her. If he had been sure that it was nothing more than an overdeveloped sex drive on his part, it wouldn't have bothered him as much as the knowledge that there were times when wanting to kiss her had no particular connection to wanting to make love to her. And that implied an emotional involvement, which scared the hell out of him.

"It looks perfect, doesn't it?" Kate sat back on her heels to admire the young tree. Sunlight caught in her hair, picking out the subtle red highlights in the brown.

"Perfect." Drew's eyes weren't on the tree.

"I think it's exactly what this corner of the yard needed."

"Exactly."

What a time to discover he was in love. The thought had him shooting to his feet, his pulse too quick, something akin to panic making his breathing a little ragged. He wasn't, of course. In love. Not with Kate. Not with anyone. He cared for her. It was safe to admit that much. He could even stretch a point and say that it was part of his job to care for her. Though he'd cared for her in ways that weren't in any training manuals on witness protection.

Drew jammed his fingers through his hair, unconcerned that they were still covered in dirt. He wasn't in love with Kate. He refused to be.

"Drew?" From Kate's tone, it was obvious that it wasn't the first time she'd said his name. He shoved his tangled thoughts aside and forced himself to focus on Kate's anxious expression.

"Are you all right?"

"Fine." He smiled, drawing on every bit of acting skill he'd picked up from years of undercover work. "My mind was wandering."

"Don't you think the tree looks just right?" she said again, accepting his explanation at face value. She slid her arm through his and looked at the young tree as if she were a proud parent admiring a clever child.

"It looks fine." Drew glanced at the old sycamore that dominated the other corner of the yard and then looked back at the sapling. "It looks a little scrawny, doesn't it?"

"In a few years it will fill out. Even by next spring, you'll be able to see a lot of growth."

"We won't be here next spring."

He felt the impact of the bare statement in the way Kate's hand tightened on his arm, heard it in the odd little catch in her breathing. He wanted to take the words back, and at the same time he felt as if he should say them again, louder this time.

"It doesn't matter," she said after a moment, her voice quiet. "It doesn't matter whether I'm here to see it or not. I'll know it's here, growing. That's good enough."

Drew looked at the tree, suddenly seeing it through Kate's eyes, seeing the hope and promise of it. It was a gift to the future, one given freely, without expectations, without conditions.

"I'm never going to be able to go back, am I?" Kate asked suddenly. "To my old life, I mean. No matter what happens at the trial. Whether Davis goes to prison or not, I won't be safe, will I?" There was no fear in her voice, no anger, just a question and an acceptance of the answer to that question.

Drew's fingers curled into a fist at his side. He would have given his life to have been able to tell her that she was wrong, that everything could go back to the way it had once been. But he couldn't lie to her.

"Davis is a powerful man," he said slowly. "Going to prison won't destroy that power completely."

"I guess I'd better start thinking about new places to live," she said lightly. But her voice wavered slightly at the end, revealing the fear under the bravado.

"Don't." Drew put his fingers under her chin, tilting her face up to his, his eyes bright blue and fierce. "You don't have to testify, Kate."

Kate caught her breath, her eyes searching his face. She knew how he felt about seeing Davis brought to justice. And yet he was telling her that she didn't have to testify, knowing what that would mean to the case—the case against the man who'd had his partner murdered.

She felt something blossom in her chest, something so fragile she hardly dared to breathe for fear of damaging it. Maybe, just maybe, Drew Hunter cared for her. Since realizing her own feelings for him, the thought had been in the back of her mind, but she'd rarely allowed it to creep into her consciousness. But if Drew could say what he had, then surely she could dare to hope...

"Even if I didn't testify, he already knows I talked to the police. He'd want to make sure I didn't change my mind in the future."

She was only pointing out what he already knew. It had been crazy to suggest that she back out now. There could be no going back. Drew reached up to brush back a lock of hair that had escaped from her ponytail.

"It's going to be all right." He said it with such total assurance that Kate could almost believe that his saying it made it the truth.

"I'd do it again," she said, her eyes clear and steady, without regrets.

"Does it mean so much to you to see Davis punished?" There was an odd combination of pride and anger in the question.

It means that much to me to know you. But she didn't say the words out loud.

"I can't just forget what I know about him," she said, giving him part of the truth. "Somebody has to try and stop him.

Drew looked down at her, unable to argue, unwilling to agree. It wasn't that he didn't want to see Davis ground into the dirt. A few months ago, he'd have sworn that he'd use any weapon to destroy the man who'd killed his partner. But he hadn't known Kate then.

Half-afraid of what she might read in his eyes, he bent to kiss her. Her mouth was soft under his, warm and welcoming. Her arms circled his waist as she tilted her head back to deepen the kiss.

There was passion in the kiss, the hunger that always lay between them, never sated. But there was something more there—a tenderness, a need, something that might almost have been a promise. Unspoken. Undefined. It was enough to make Kate's heart beat just a little faster, to make the fragile hope she nurtured grow a little stronger.

"Hey, you two! None of that. Bill's about to throw the steaks on." Jane's cheery voice sailed over the waist-high fence that separated the two yards.

Drew and Kate ended their kiss without haste. For a moment, Kate looked into Drew's eyes, trying to read what he was feeling. But the combination of twilight and his natural tendency to conceal his thoughts defeated her. Whatever Drew felt for her—if anything—she could read nothing in his face.

"Come on, lovebirds. Dinner awaits." Jane's laughing order banished any lingering fragments of the tender moment between them.

Smiling, Kate turned to wave at her, wondering if Drew felt as she did that they'd been on the verge of discovering something about each other, about whatever it was that lay between them. And she wondered whether he was glad or sorry that the moment had been broken.

FAMILY BARBECUES were not something with which Drew had had much experience. He'd never considered himself the backyard barbecue type. But then, he'd been doing a lot of things lately that he'd never imagined himself doing. Things like making love to a witness he was supposed to be protecting.

At least enjoying the barbecue wasn't likely to get him kicked off the force, he thought, finding a kind of black humor in the thought. Later he'd wonder at how little it bothered him to think about the mess he'd be in if it came out that he'd taken his role as Kate's husband so much to heart. For now he intended to enjoy himself.

It wasn't difficult. Jane and Bill Dumont were pleasant company. After nearly twenty years of marriage, they were so closely attuned that, often, one would start a sentence and the other would finish it.

Kate found herself watching the two of them quarrel good-naturedly over who had to take the blame for the fact that the steaks had been cooked considerably past the stage where they could be labeled rare. Even in the midst of a disagreement, they were obviously two halves of the same whole, a tightly knit unit that required no outside input to sustain it.

But they were generous about bringing others into their circle, commenting on Kate's work in the yard, asking Drew about his novel. Kate wasn't surprised to hear Drew discuss the progress on his nonexistent book. She suspected he could probably quote a passage or two if someone demanded it. He was nothing if not thoroughly prepared for this role.

It was not an entirely comforting thought, she admitted, frowning down at her plate. No wonder it was so difficult to read anything of what he was thinking. He was so good at hiding who he really was that it had become habit.

"Actually, this is by way of a celebration," Bill announced, drawing Kate's attention away from pondering the difficulties of falling in love with a man who'd been trained to lie for a living.

"A celebration?" Drew lifted one brow questioningly, his mouth curved in a lazy smile. No one looking at him would ever think he was anything other than what he was pretending to be—a mild-mannered teacher on sabbatical. The thought of how far that was from the truth made Kate feel suddenly very uncertain.

"What are we celebrating?" she asked, forcing herself to put aside the thought that, while she might be in love with Drew, she wasn't at all sure she really knew him.

"Do you want to tell them?" Bill asked his wife.

"You can break the news. You're the one who's so all-fired smug about it." Jane's grin made it clear that she was feeling a trifle smug herself.

"Well, one of you tell us before curiosity does us in," Drew said, laughing.

"In approximately six and one-half months, we're going to be rediscovering the joys of 2:00 a.m. feedings, no sleep and dirty diapers," Bill announced, looking both excited and slightly embarrassed.

It took a few seconds for his meaning to sink in and then Kate and Drew both spoke at once, offering their congratulations and asking questions. Jane was flushed with pleasure, admitting that she'd never thought she'd want another child until it had suddenly occurred to her that time was running out on her option to try.

"How does Kenny feel about the prospect of having a baby brother or sister?" Drew asked. He grinned when Bill groaned and rolled his eyes in an obvious imitation of Kenny's response.

"He was horrified to think his parents were still capable of procreating," Jane said. She laughed. "He seemed to think it was going to cause him great embarrassment with his friends when they realized that we must have done something more than sleep together for me to get in this condition."

"He'll get over it," Kate said.

"Yeah, but wait until he finds out that he's expected to change diapers," Bill said.

"Can't say I blame him on that one," Drew said, shuddering theatrically.

"Just wait until the two of you start hearing the patter of little feet," Jane said. "Kate'll have you trained in no time."

Kate laughed, but she was careful not to look at Drew. The thought of having his child was suddenly an ache inside her.

"I think we're going to wait awhile," Drew said, and Kate wondered if it was only her imagination that made it seem as if his good humor was just a little forced.

"You've got plenty of time." Bill set his arm around his wife's shoulders and hugged her close. "Janey and I started early with Kenny and there were times we wished we'd had a few more years with just the two of us."

"Not that we ever regretted having Kenny," Jane added hastily.

"He's a great kid," Drew said.

"We think he's okay," Bill admitted with a grin. "But you two, you've only been married, what? A few months?"

"That's right." Drew glanced at Kate and smiled. "Just a few months."

Kate smiled back at him, wishing it weren't all lies. They did it so well, she thought, presented such a perfect image of a happy couple, their marriage still new and fresh. She'd have just about given her soul to make the image a reality. She was relieved when the conversation veered away from a discussion of babies and marriages. Neither topic was a particular favorite of hers at the moment.

Kate had brought her guitar, and she got it out after supper. They'd spent several evenings with the Dumonts and they almost always ended up the same way, with the four of them singing folk songs and laughing.

Drew had been surprised by Kate's skill on the guitar. She was no Segovia, but she had a good feel for the instrument. She tilted her head toward the neck of the guitar, her hair swinging forward to half conceal her face as she strummed the opening chords for "Tom Dooley." They all sang, mangling the verses occasionally, humming when they forgot the words.

He'd never in his life been part of such a gathering, never imagined himself a part of one. Which made it all the more amazing that he felt so completely at home. Amazing and just a little scary.

The small gathering broke up shortly before ten. The Dumonts walked to the edge of their property with Drew and Kate, commenting on the beauty of the summer night. The two couples parted at the sidewalk, exchanging quiet good-nights and more congratulations.

When they reached their own front porch, Kate glanced back and saw Bill and Jane entering their house. His arm was around her, his head bent over hers. There was so much tenderness in the way he held her, so much love, that Kate felt tears sting her eyes.

"I'm tired," Kate said as the door closed behind them. "I think I'll get ready for bed."

"I'll be in as soon as I've locked everything up," Drew said. He set her guitar case in the living room.

They sounded just like an old married couple, Kate thought as she made her way to the bedroom they'd shared for the past two weeks. It was so easy to forget that it was all a charade, an elaborate game they were playing to keep her alive.

She went into the bathroom and took a quick shower. The bedroom was still empty when she entered. Drew had probably stopped to watch a bit of the late news. Kate wondered suddenly if there'd come a time when *she* was part of the news, but she quickly shoved the thought away. There was nothing to be gained by thinking like that.

And yet it wasn't possible *not* to think of how her life had changed. Today she'd finally faced the fact that she could never go back to her apartment, never call it home again. Tonight she realized that there were other things she'd given up, things she'd never even thought of.

She was sitting on the side of the bed when Drew came in, running a brush through her hair, her eyes focused on nothing at all.

"You were quiet tonight," Drew commented as he toed off his shoes in front of the closet. Kate blinked once or twice, as if having trouble shifting her thoughts. She shrugged lightly.

"I was just thinking about how close Jane and Bill are. They've been together so long, it's almost like they're two halves of the same person." Kate shook her head wonderingly. "I can't imagine what it must feel like to be that close to someone."

Drew paused in the act of unbuttoning his shirt and looked at her. There'd been an odd little ache in her voice, a kind of yearning.

"I guess after twenty years together, you tend to get pretty close to someone."

"Not always. My mother and I lived together for eighteen years and we were never more than reluctant roommates. She couldn't wait until I was old enough for her to get on with her life." There was no bitterness in her words, just acceptance of what had been.

"Well, Jane and Bill seem happy together," he said, choosing not to comment on her relationship with her mother. He was afraid if he said anything, it would be something harsh. It struck him as ironic that *he* should feel critical of someone who was incapable of love.

"It's wonderful about the baby, isn't it? They're so happy about it." Kate's voice was wistful.

"Two o'clock feedings and all," he agreed. He pulled his T-shirt off over his head and was reaching for the snap at the waist of his jeans when she spoke again.

"I'll never be able to have children, will I?"

"Why not?" Drew's head came up, his eyes sharp and questioning.

"Because I'm never going to be safe again. I'll always be looking over my shoulder, wondering if Davis is about to catch up with me, to punish me for speaking up."

"Don't think like that." His voice was sharper than he'd intended, made so by the image her words conjured up.

"If I ever had a family, they'd be in danger, too," she continued as if he hadn't spoken. "I couldn't live with that, couldn't live with the idea that something might happen to a child—my child— because I'd testified against Davis."

Drew covered the few feet between them and took hold of her shoulders, drawing her to her feet. His grip was uncomfortably tight.

"Your life isn't over just because you're testifying."

"Not over. Just . . . changed." She forced a smile she didn't feel and lifted her shoulders in a shrug, the movement hampered by the pressure of his fingers. "Hey, I'd probably make a lousy mother, anyway."

The small wobble in her voice was hardly audible, but Drew heard it. His fingers tightened on her shoulders for an instant and then he pulled her forward to lean against his chest, slipping his arms around her back. Anger tightened his throat, choking off anything he might have said. It was a self-directed anger.

He hadn't given much thought to what it was going to cost to nail Davis. He'd known that Kate was putting her life at risk. That was the reason for his being here, to protect her. But he hadn't really thought beyond the trial, beyond the anticipated pleasure of hearing Davis declared guilty.

He was only now realizing just how large a price Kate might have to pay for having a conscience. More than he'd ever wanted anything in his life, he wanted to be able to tell her that she was wrong— wrong about not being able to go back to her old life, wrong about having to look over her shoulder. But it would have been a lie.

"It's going to be all right, Kate." It was a promise he had no power to keep and they both knew it. But it made him feel a little less powerless to say it, made her feel a little less frightened to hear it.

"Maybe we'll get lucky and Davis will offend some hardened criminal once he's in prison and our problem will be solved," Drew offered.

Kate's snort of laughter was muffled against his chest. She wondered if he knew he'd linked them together—maybe *we'll* get lucky. It made it sound as if he planned on being around after the trial, as if whatever it was they had together wasn't going to end the instant they set foot inside Los Angeles County.

"I won't let anything happen to you, Kate."

Another promise he might not be able to keep, but it didn't matter. What mattered was that he cared enough to make it. And caring could become loving, given time and nurture. She was willing to provide the nurturing, but she had the sad feeling that time might be denied her. But there was nothing she could do about it now. Now all she could do was what she'd been doing for weeks—live only in the moment.

And pray that moment would last forever.

She felt his breath against her forehead and closed her eyes, letting him tilt her head back against his shoulder. His mouth brushed over her eyelids as if drying the tears she refused to shed. He tasted the soft curve of her cheek, the hollow behind her ear, the delicate line of her jaw. By the time his lips touched hers, Kate felt as if he'd soothed all her hurts, smothered all her worries. As long as Drew was kissing her like this, nothing else seemed to matter.

She shifted in his arms, her arms lifting to circle his shoulders, her fingers burrowing into the thick black hair at the back of his neck. Her mouth opened to him, her tongue coming up to fence delicately with his. Drew flattened one hand against her lower back, urging her closer, letting her feel the pressure of his arousal through the layers of cloth that separated them.

In the short time since they'd become lovers, Kate thought she'd experienced just about every nuance of lovemaking possible. Drew had made love to her gently, almost coaxing her response, drawing out each moment until she thought she'd go mad. He'd also shown her that sex could be fierce and quick and just as satisfying. Tonight he made love to her with such tenderness that it brought tears to her eyes.

He eased her nightgown over her head, discarding it in a soft white pool on the carpet. His fingers trailed lightly over her breasts, his thumbs just brushing the taut peaks but not lingering to satisfy. He let his hands slide over her warm skin, the light, skimming touch setting fire to nerve endings she'd barely known existed. And all the while, his mouth lingered on hers, stealing away what little breath she had.

Somewhere in the back of her mind, Kate thought that she shouldn't let him distract her with sex. But she dismissed the thought. Tonight she wanted—needed—his touch, as if it could reaffirm her belief that things could work out. She thought of how foolish it was to lie to herself.

But it wasn't long before she wasn't thinking anything at all.

Drew eased her down onto the bed, bracing one knee against the mattress as he lowered her. Supporting his weight on his arms, he kissed her, a light, teasing kiss that added fuel to the fire burning low in her belly. He nibbled his way down the length of her throat, pausing to let his tongue feel the flutter of the pulse at its base.

Then his lips were brushing over her nipples. She arched, her fingers digging into his shoulder in a silent plea. She thought she felt him smile against her and then his mouth was opening over her, drawing her inside.

His fingers brushed over her stomach, finding the triangle of dark, curling hair at the top of her thighs. Kate whimpered softly as he found the moist heat of her. He switched his attention to her other breast, laving the nipple with his tongue before drawing it into his mouth. And all the while, his fingers were discovering the hidden secrets of her.

She moaned a protest when he left her and then felt his hands close around her hips. She arched, her thighs opening to cradle his hips, her body aching to be filled. But what she felt was not the hard pressure of his masculinity. It was a soft kiss, delicate as a butterfly's wing yet sending shock waves through her body.

"Drew!" Whether his name was protest or welcome, she couldn't have said. Her hands came down, her fingers burrowing into his hair. But if she'd intended to push him away, the intention flew out the window when she felt his tongue against the very heart of her.

She arched into his intimate kiss, her breath leaving her on a sob. She felt as if she were slowly breaking into a thousand different pieces. Never in her life had she imagined the intensity of the sensations he sent rocketing through her.

He played her as if she were a fine instrument, gauging her reactions perfectly, making her shiver with pleasure and sob his name as wave after wave of sensation washed over her. And just when she thought she couldn't stand another moment, he showed her how wrong she was.

He rose above her, his hands braced on either side of her head. Looking up into his face, Kate felt hunger stir anew, though she'd have sworn it wasn't possible. Reaching between them, she closed her fingers around his tumescent length, feeling a wave of feminine triumph when he shuddered at the sweet pain of her touch.

Her eyes locked on his, she drew him forward. He rested against her a moment, barely touching her, teasing them both with the thought of what lay ahead. And then he thrust forward, sheathing himself in her welcoming body.

Kate closed her eyes, drawing her legs up to cradle him more fully, savoring the feelings of completeness. This was what she'd spent a lifetime waiting for.

It could not last long. The fever heat couldn't be sustained. The heat built with each movement, the fire growing hotter and hotter until it was scorching. And then the flames burst out of control, consuming them, completing them, joining them fully.

Kate cradled Drew's heavy weight against her, closing her eyes against the sting of tears. She loved him. Heart and soul, forever and always. How much time did they have left? A week, a few days? Long enough for him to come to love her?

Please, God, just a few more days. A few more memories to store up against what might be a lifetime without him. Surely that wasn't too much to ask.

Chapter Ten

Drew was wide-awake before the echoes of the first ring had faded. The phone rang again, a sharp electronic demand for attention, shattering the quiet. A glance at the clock told him it was not quite seven. Not an hour at which anyone was likely to be calling to try and sell something.

"Whaisit?" Sleep blurred the words together as Kate lifted her head from his shoulder.

"The phone," he said. A third ring punctuated his words.

She blinked and he felt the sudden tension in her body as she registered the early hour and obviously came to the same conclusion he had about the caller's identity.

"It could be a wrong number," she said.

Drew didn't bother to answer her. He knew as well as she did that it wasn't a wrong number. Rolling away from her, he swung his legs over the side of the bed and picked up the phone in the middle of the fourth ring.

"Hello."

Let it be a wrong number, Kate prayed, crossing her fingers in a childish plea for good luck. *Please, please, please. Not now. Not after last night. Not when she was just starting to believe he might come to love her. No man could make love to a woman with such tenderness if he didn't feel something for her. Just a little while longer. A few more days. A week. She just wanted a little more time. That wasn't so much to ask for.*

But it was more than she was going to get. Drew wasn't hanging up, wasn't suggesting that the caller might have made a mistake in dialing. He wasn't even mentioning that six forty-five was a ridiculous hour for a phone call.

Feeling as if breathing suddenly required a conscious effort, Kate sat up, drawing the sheet up over her breasts, staring at Drew's back, listening to his end of the conversation. It was brief and told her very little. He said "yes" twice, stopped and listened and then said, "Tomorrow." There was another pause and then he repeated the word, his tone flat and hard.

"Tomorrow." There was another pause and then, "Fine."

Kate watched him hang up the phone, her eyes following the motion of his hand as if it were important that she see the receiver settle into the base.

For the space of several slow heartbeats, Drew didn't move. He sat with his back to her, his hand still on the phone. It was so quiet, she almost thought that it was possible to hear the rush of blood in her veins, the thrum of it pulsing in her temples.

Finally he turned to look at her. She felt his eyes on her, but she couldn't seem to shift her gaze from the plain black phone on the night table. It was a stupid place to put a phone, she thought. Why did people put phones next to their beds. No one wanted to wake to the shrill jangle of it ringing. And you weren't even alert enough to hold a decent conversation if it did wake you. Not that Drew had sounded anything less than coherent. But she wouldn't have expected anything...

"They need you back in L.A. tomorrow."

The flat statement sent her thoughts skittering in a thousand different directions. But they all came back to one resting place.

It was over.

Just what "it" was, she couldn't have said. Her time with Drew, the whole charade. Her life. One of them or all of them. She wasn't sure it mattered.

She drew a deep breath and looked at him at last. All the gold seemed drained from her eyes, leaving them dull green and lifeless. Her mouth twisted upward as if struggling for a smile, but it couldn't quite make it.

"I guess I'd better get started packing," she said.

Drew opened his mouth and then shut it without speaking. There wasn't anything to say. He watched Kate bend down to lift her nightgown from the floor where it had been discarded the night before. She pulled it over her head, letting it drop around her hips when she stood.

He'd never understand what it was about that plain white cotton nightgown that always made him think of hot nights and hotter sex. If he never saw her again, he'd always remember that nightgown. The sound of the bathroom door closing behind her cut the thought off.

If he never saw her again.

Drew closed his eyes, afraid that the words just might be prophetic. Even more afraid that his life wouldn't be worth living if they were.

IT TURNED OUT TO BE amazingly easy to dismantle the facade they'd created. Kate packed her things, feeling as if it had been a hundred years ago that she'd first done this. That had been another woman, someone she hardly knew anymore.

She stopped, her fingers tightening on the half-finished quilt top she'd been folding. It wasn't just the possibility that Davis might try to extract revenge for her testimony that made it impossible for her to go back to her old life. It was the fact that she'd changed. She wasn't the same Kate Sloane who'd carefully built herself a cozy little nest in that apartment.

After spending all her life moving from place to place, never feeling as if anywhere was really home, she'd been determined to create a home for herself. And she thought she'd accomplished that. Surrounded by things she'd chosen, staying in one place as the months and years rolled by, she'd thought she finally had what she'd always wanted— a home.

It was only now that it was lost to her that she realized it had been more cocoon than home. She'd wrapped herself in quilting fabric and domesticity and told herself she was content. And perhaps she had been. But she'd only been half-alive.

Falling in love had shown her how incomplete her life had been before. Home wasn't just a place, it was a feeling. It was a feeling of completeness, of being whole. With Drew she was complete.

The most annoying thing about truisms was that they were almost always true. Home, at least for her, really was where the heart is. Her heart was with Drew. She only wished she knew where his was.

BY TWO O'CLOCK, they were on the road. The keys to the house had been returned to Jane. Drew had explained that his mother was ill and they were rushing to her bedside. Jane had been sympathetic and said that she hoped his mother recovered quickly and that she'd take care of the garden until they returned. Kate bit the inside of her lip until she tasted blood, hating the lies.

She couldn't stop herself from looking at the little house as Drew backed the car out of the driveway. She'd known some of the happiest moments of her life here and she'd never see it again. She hoped Jane would remember to water the roses and the tree she and Drew had planted—God, was that only yesterday?

Blinking against the sudden sting of tears, she turned her eyes resolutely forward, refusing to look back.

THEY SPOKE VERY little. Drew kept his eyes on the road, as if driving took up every bit of his concentration. Kate didn't even bother to get out a quilt block to work on, though her tote was at her feet. The handwork had helped soothe her nerves on the drive up the coast, but it was going to take more than that to distract her this time.

Before, they'd taken a roundabout route north, hoping to discourage anyone who might have followed them. This time, Drew picked up Highway 5, right through the middle of the state. It was a route known for its speed rather than its scenic attractions. Staring out the window at miles of nothing, Kate tried very hard not to think of anything at all.

She must have succeeded fairly well, because somewhere around the middle of the state she managed to fall asleep. When she woke, it was dark and Drew was pulling off the highway. Sitting up, Kate brushed her hair back from her face and rubbed her eyes, feeling disoriented.

"Where are we?"

"Ventura County. We'll spend the night here and go into L.A. in the morning. Lavery is meeting us at the courthouse."

"We could finish the trip tonight," she pointed out, glancing at the clock in the dashboard. They were just above Los Angeles.

"I told Lavery we'd be there tomorrow." He flicked on the turn signal and turned into the parking lot of a motel that had a vacancy sign flashing out front.

"Did he want us there today?" Kate asked, remembering his side of the phone conversation and his adamant repetition of the word "tomorrow."

"I figured tomorrow was soon enough."

And that was all the explanation she was going to get, Kate thought, reading his tone. He wasn't going to tell her why he'd decided that tomorrow was soon enough. Would she be a fool to hope that part of the reason he'd insisted on the extra few hours was because he wanted to spend them with her?

"You hungry?" he asked as he shut off the engine.

"I guess I should be." Kate ran her fingers through her hair, putting it in slightly tousled order. There was a hollow feeling in her stomach, but she didn't think it had anything to do with hunger.

"There's a coffee shop. Why don't you order us something while I get a room."

Kate ordered bowls of soup and added a sandwich for Drew. The food arrived at the same time he did and they ate in near silence. Kate kept thinking about how little time was left. A few hours and they'd be back in Los Angeles.

Drew paid for their meal and they walked to the room he'd rented, still without speaking. Kate's thoughts tumbled one over the other. What if he handed her over to his boss or whomever was in charge of witnesses at a trial and then just disappeared from her life forever? What if he was immediately given another assignment?

The room was typical of a motel. Beige walls, beige carpets, beige bedspreads and curtains. There were two cheaply framed floral prints on the wall, but they were swallowed up in the sheer beigeness of their surroundings. Not that Kate would have noticed if it had been the Ritz. She wasn't interested in their surroundings, wasn't interested in anything but what was going to happen tomorrow.

"I love you." She hadn't planned to say the words, hadn't even realized that was what she was going to say when she opened her mouth.

They had stopped at the car to get what luggage they'd need for the night. Her tote and Drew's duffel hit the floor with soft thuds as if his fingers had just gone numb. She stared at his back and felt no regret at having finally said what had been locked inside her for weeks.

"I love you, Drew. I don't expect you to say it back. I just had to tell you how I felt. I don't know what's going to happen tomorrow, whether or not I'll see you after that. I don't even know whether or not you'll *want* to see me. And it's okay if you don't." She forced a smile as he slowly turned to face her.

"Kate—"

"Really, it's all right if you don't," she rushed into speech, terrified of what he might say—of what he might *not* say. "I'm not telling you how I feel to make you feel guilty or obligated. It's not your fault I fell in love with you."

"Kate—"

"And don't tell me all about how I'm just imagining it because we spent a lot of time together and I had to depend on you to protect me. Because I thought of that. And that's not what this is. But I don't expect anything from you. And I'm not going to make any demands."

"Kate, I—"

"And you don't have to worry about me making any kind of scenes or letting anyone find out about what happened between us. I know it would get you in a lot of trouble. So once we get to L.A., I'll act like nothing happened between us."

"Kate, would you—"

"I'd just like to ask one favor." She knew she was babbling, but she couldn't seem to stop talking. If she slowed down, he might say something. And, at the moment, that scared her more than anything. "I guess the police are still going to want someone to protect me and I'd like it to be you. I don't know if I can make requests like that, but I could just tell them it was because I'm used to you. Like an old shoe."

"An old shoe?" Drew had momentarily given up trying to get a real response in. He was watching her with those ice blue eyes, his expression unreadable, as usual.

"Of course, maybe you'd rather I *didn't* ask if you could stay with me. Maybe you'd like to go on to something else. I wouldn't mind." Her voice trembled slightly on the bald-faced lie, but she steadied it immediately. "I know you've got a career to think about and I wouldn't—"

Drew stopped her by the simple expedient of pulling her into his arms and covering her mouth with his. For an instant, Kate was stiff in his hold. But a heartbeat later, she'd melted against him, her fingers curling into his shirt, clinging to him as if he were the only solid thing in the world.

Passion flared quick and hard. Suddenly the layers of clothing that separated them were too much to be tolerated. Drew's hands were impatient with Kate's shirt and she heard a seam rip. Her own fingers were occupied with trying to work his belt buckle loose.

Since the early-morning call that had destroyed the fragile facade they'd created, tension had been building in each of them. Suddenly everything had shifted. Nothing was what it had been. The past was a fantasy and the future an uncertainty. Only the present mattered, only the feel of Drew's hands on her skin, the welcome pressure of his body on hers as they tumbled to the bed.

They made love like lovers long parted, still half-dressed, clothing wrenched open and pushed out of the way. Kate cried out a welcome when Drew's hard strength filled her. Drew groaned at the feeling of her soft warmth cradling him.

It was quick and hard, ending much too soon and yet leaving shock waves that seemed to go on forever. Kate clung to Drew's shoulders, listening to the ragged beat of his heart, feeling him still a part of her. He hadn't said the words, hadn't told her he loved her. But surely he'd told her with his body. He couldn't make love to her with such hunger if he didn't love her.

She shifted slightly, drawing her knees up against his hips to cradle him more fully, her fingers tracing the length of his spine under his opened shirt. She caught her breath as she felt him stir inside her, his hunger no more sated than her own.

They managed to get the rest of their clothes off this time, stripping back the covers to tumble onto the cool sheets. It was slower but no less powerful. The waves of completion were harder, deeper, seeming to rock endlessly through her body.

Kate's nails dug into his back, her neck arching as she was swept up on the crest of a wave and then plunged wildly into the heart of a storm. Drew's mouth swallowed her sobs of pleasure, his own body taut and hard above her.

Afterward Kate fell asleep as quickly and easily as a child. The day had taken a toll on her and she mumbled sleepily as Drew gently pulled away from her and settled on the bed, drawing her to his side. She was asleep instantly, her head snuggled into his shoulder, one leg thrown across his hips.

Sleep did not come as easily to Drew. He stared up at the dark ceiling, hearing her tell him she loved him. Hearing his own silence in answer.

Why hadn't he said something? Anything. Why had he stood there like a wax dummy, listening to her, seeing the fear and need in her eyes and not saying a word. Because the words he should have said had stuck in his throat, refusing to come out.

I love you. Three one-syllable words. What could be easier?

What could be harder?

THE WORDS DIDN'T COME any easier in the cool light of morning.

They'd awakened in the night, reaching for each other, making love with a kind of quiet desperation. Afterward Drew cradled Kate against his chest, wanting to give her the words she needed to hear and unable to force them out.

THE DRIVE TO L.A. was quiet. Each was wrapped in their own thoughts. Kate felt as if there were a million things she wanted to say before it was too late, but she couldn't think of any of them. She'd expected to feel self-conscious with him this morning, expected to feel uneasy that he hadn't responded to her declaration of love. There was none of that.

When she thought about it, she knew it was because, in her mind at least, he had answered her. He'd answered her with his body. And if it was naive of her to believe that he couldn't have made love to her the way he had if he didn't love her, then she was content to hold on to her naiveté.

They reached the outskirts of the sprawl that was Los Angeles and Kate felt her stomach tighten. The glass of juice and roll she'd had for breakfast suddenly felt like brick. Soon they'd be meeting with Lieutenant Lavery and Drew would be handing over his responsibility for her. Only, she'd already bet her heart on being much more than just a responsibility to him.

She slid a glance sideways at his profile. There was nothing to be read, unless she could read something significant in the fact that his jaw seemed made of granite or in the little muscle that ticked restlessly at the outer corner of his eye.

Sensing her eyes on him, he took his gaze off the road long enough to send her a quick look. At least she no longer had to worry that her heart might be in her eyes, she thought. Her mouth quirked in a self-deprecating smile. She'd always been a lousy poker player, anyway.

"We're almost there." Drew's quiet announcement sent a jolt of panic spiraling through her. Her fingers knotted together in her lap and she took a deep breath, trying to still the frantic beat of her heart. He flicked on the turn signal and turned into the parking lot.

"The courthouse is about half a block that way," he said, nodding his head to their left. "Just in case Davis has people waiting for us, we'll park here and go in a back way. I called in a favor this morning and someone will be waiting to let us in through the basement."

"Okay." She couldn't make it seem real. He was talking about the possibility that someone might be waiting to kill her. She'd had weeks to adjust to the idea, but it still didn't seem to have any direct application to her.

She reached for the door handle, but Drew's hand caught her forearm. Turning back to look at him, she saw his eyes, bright and fierce with an emotion she didn't quite dare to name.

"It's going to be all right, Kate. *You're* going to be all right."

"I know." She didn't know anything anymore except that this man had become her life. She tried to force a smile, but Drew leaned across the car and kissed her, quick and hard.

"I'll stay with you as long as they'll let me. Lavery may insist on assigning someone else to protect you, but I'll do my best."

"Thank you."

"It's what I want." He pulled open his car door and got out before Kate could ask if *she* was part of what he wanted.

She got out of the car. Drew was waiting for her at the rear fender. His eyes scanned the half-empty parking lot, looking for anything that seemed out of place. Apparently he was satisfied with what he saw because he set his hand against Kate's back and urged her forward.

She'd never felt so exposed in her life. The parking lot seemed more like the Gobi Desert, huge, empty and exposed. She wanted nothing so much as to reach out and take hold of Drew's hand, holding it for comfort. But of course she couldn't do anything of the sort.

From now on, she had to think of him as a police officer. He'd never said anything about it, but she didn't doubt that if anyone ever found out they were lovers, he'd almost certainly lose his job.

There'd be no explaining how right it had been, that he hadn't taken advantage of her.

So she walked beside him, trying to look as calm as he did, wishing she could turn and run for the safety of the car and then take the car and leave the city behind forever.

Drew could feel her trembling, could sense her fear. He wanted nothing so much as to put his arm around her, hold her close and tell her that she never had to be afraid of anything again. Even better would be to take her back to the car and just get in and drive away. To hell with Davis. Let someone else be the sacrificial lamb on this particular altar of justice. All he cared about was Kate, keeping her safe.

"There's an alley just past that building on the right. We'll cut through there and come in behind the courthouse."

"Okay." Kate barely heard him; she was too busy trying to force enough strength into her knees to keep her upright.

"Detective Hunter?" The man stepped out from behind a van. Drew pushed Kate behind him, his hand reaching inside his jacket for his shoulder holster. Seeing the blue uniform the man wore slowed the motion, but he didn't relax his stance.

"I'm Officer Williams, Detective." He looked very serious, very official. Drew's hand remained inside his jacket, though he'd not yet drawn his gun. His eyes skimmed the area behind the officer.

"What are you doing here?" he asked at last.

"Lieutenant Lavery sent me to escort Ms. Sloane to the courthouse. He was delayed."

"Delayed? What happened?"

Kate obeyed the subtle motion of his shoulder and edged farther behind him. She didn't know what was wrong. Officer Williams looked genuine. He looked just like the policeman who'd visited her elementary class one year and talked about traffic safety. He had the sort of square-jawed, not-too-handsome face that inspired trust.

"The lieutenant had car trouble on the way here. He radioed the station and asked that someone be sent to meet you." Williams's hand moved slightly, a hardly noticeable motion that happened to put it a little closer to his holstered gun.

"The hell he did." Drew reached back with his left hand, catching Kate's shoulder and shoving her between two parked cars. Caught off balance, she stumbled and fell to her knees, feeling the hard asphalt scrape her skin through her slacks. There were shots—two, three? She threw her hands over her ears as the sounds seemed to echo inside her head.

And then Drew was beside her, grabbing her arm, shaking her, demanding to know if she was all right.

"I'm fine." She blinked, looking past his shoulder to focus on the uniformed leg she could see in the gap between the cars. It was ominously still.

"Is he dead?" She realized she'd whispered the question, a ridiculous precaution considering the amount of noise the shots had made.

"I don't know. He won't be bothering us again." Drew was levering fresh bullets into the clip on his .38, unconcerned with whether or not Williams was dead. "Lavery didn't send him. He wouldn't risk sending someone else, but if he had, there's a code. And this guy didn't know the code."

"Maybe he forgot." Kate hardly knew what she was saying. She couldn't take her eyes from that leg. "He looked like a real policeman."

"He probably was." He ignored her gasp of shock. "This was clumsy. They must not have had much time to set this up." He frowned at a dent in the gray door behind Kate's head. "We'll go back to the car. Get the hell out of here. Then I can get hold of Lavery and find out what happened."

"Are there more of them?" Kate was pleasantly surprised that her voice was level.

"Probably. Stay down. We'll try to stay between the cars. If I tell you to do something, you do it immediately. Don't stop to question me."

"Okay." She nodded, acknowledging the logic of that.

Drew would have liked to say something to erase the fear from her eyes, but there was nothing he could say.

Keeping to a crouch, Kate followed Drew as he eased his way around the parked cars. Adrenaline pumped through her, keeping screaming fear at bay, keeping her head clear. Once they were out of this, she would probably collapse completely, she thought, but for the moment she was holding on to her control, even if it was only by the skin of her teeth.

"Damn."

She crept up behind Drew, looking over his shoulder at the gap between them, and the welcome familiarity of the sedan they'd parked just a few minutes before. There were ten yards of bare asphalt between them and safety. It looked like a thousand.

"We're going to run for it. You go first. I'll be right behind you. Open the driver's door and slide over into the passenger seat. Get the key in the ignition." He reached into his pocket and pulled out the keys, pressing them into her hand. "I'll be right behind you."

"Okay."

"Don't stop if you hear shooting, and if something happens to me you keep going."

"But—"

"No. There're no buts. If something happens to me, you take the car and drive like hell. Go to the courthouse. Drive up the damn steps if you have to. Lavery will show up."

"Drew, I—"

"Just do it." He took hold of her upper arm, urging her in front of him, giving her no time to tell him any of the hundred things she wanted to say. "Keep as low as you can and run as fast as you can."

"Drew—"

"Now!"

And somehow she was running across the hot asphalt, hearing Drew's footsteps behind her. Or was that the pounding of her own heart she heard? They were going to make it, she thought. Just a little farther.

She heard a shot and the windshield next to her suddenly had a neat little hole, surrounded by a spider's web of cracks. Despite Drew's orders, she turned. Drew had stopped, dropping to one knee in a classic pose, arm out, the gun an extension of his hand. She saw him fire and jerked her head in time to see a body tumble from the top of the van where Williams had been waiting for them.

"I told you to keep going," he snarled, rising to his feet and starting toward her. Before she could find the words to defend herself, she saw a movement behind him.

"Behind you!" Drew spun, bringing up his gun. But the movement wasn't quick enough. Kate saw the impact of the bullet as it struck him in the chest. She screamed and before the sound had died, another shot struck him. He fell, tumbling back behind the front fender of a car. She was beside him in a minute, oblivious to the fact that a third bullet shattered the headlight a split second after she passed it.

Grabbing Drew under the shoulders, she dragged him a few feet until he was completely behind the car, not even feeling the strain on her arms and back as they took his weight.

She eased him down as gently as she could, unaware that she was sobbing under her breath. Blood was already soaking his jacket, making an ugly black stain on the gray linen.

"Dammit, Kate, I told you not to stop." His voice was stronger than she'd expected. Probably shock prevented him from feeling the pain. But that would wear off shortly. She had to stop the bleeding.

"I've never been much good at obeying orders," she told him. She pushed open his jacket, feeling faint when she saw the spreading stain on his white shirt.

"Well, you're going to obey this one." He reached up to catch her hand, his grip stronger than it had any right to be. "You're going to get in that car and get out of here. That guy is still out there. He's just looking for an angle to get a shot. Now go."

"No." Her eyes met his. Tears streamed down her cheeks, but there was hard determination in her look. "I'm not leaving you."

"Do as I say."

"Shut up. You're wasting your energy." She was ripping open his shirt as she spoke. "I love you, and I'm not leaving you here to bleed to death in this filthy parking lot."

"Please, Kate. Go. Please."

It was harder to fight him when she heard the weakness in his voice. But she couldn't leave him. She set her jaw.

"No."

The shock was wearing off and Drew could feel pain settling in his chest. In contrast, his left arm was numb. He was badly wounded. Maybe fatally, he thought, with complete clarity. There was nothing Kate could do here except get herself killed trying to save him. The thought of dying didn't frighten him half as much as the thought of something happening to Kate.

"You stupid little idiot." He gathered every bit of his energy and put as much contempt as he could into his voice. "I don't love you. I don't even particularly like you. You were just convenient. It helped pass the time. You don't mean a damn thing to me. Now get the hell out of here."

He saw Kate's eyes lift to his face, but his vision was starting to blur, making it impossible to see her expression. Now she'd go. She'd leave and he could at least hope that she'd get to safety.

And then she smiled at him, the radiance of the expression penetrating the fog that was starting to swallow him.

"You must love me at least a little or you wouldn't be trying so hard to get rid of me."

"I love you a lot," he said, feeling despair swallow him. "That's why you have to go. Please, Kate. Please." The last word was hardly audible.

Kate froze for a moment, her eyes on his face. But there was no time to analyze what she was feeling. No time to savor the fact that Drew had said he loved her. She heard a sound, the soft scuff of leather soles on a hard surface.

Lifting her head, she saw a tall figure step into the gap between the cars. His back was to the sun and she could make out nothing more than an outline. Her hand dropped to the asphalt, her fingers closing around the butt of her gun. Her purse was lying somewhere in the parking lot, dropped and forgotten. But she'd had the gun in her jacket pocket. She'd set it beside Drew when she'd opened his jacket and now it came into her hand as naturally as if she'd been handling it all her life.

She saw the man's arm moving, lifting toward her. There was a glint of sunlight on a gun barrel and then she lifted her hand. Pointing the gun like a finger, the way the instructor had said, she pulled the trigger. Once. Twice. A third time. And then there was nothing to shoot at. He'd fallen back on the ground and he wasn't moving.

Kate lowered the gun slowly, feeling nothing but a vague hope that it was over, that this was the last of them.

"I told you I'd do what I had to if the time came," she said. But when she looked down at Drew, she saw that he was unconscious. Blood still pooled from the wounds on his chest, spreading at a frightening rate.

"Don't you dare die on me, Drew Hunter," she muttered under her breath. Ripping buttons in her haste, she stripped her blouse off, folding it into a pad and pressing it against the wound that seemed to be bleeding the most. She could hear the wail of sirens nearby.

She knelt beside Drew, oblivious to the fact that she was just wearing torn slacks and a bra, keeping the makeshift pressure pad against his chest, waiting for the police to find them and praying that it wouldn't be too late.

It couldn't be too late.

IF SHE LIVED HERE for a thousand years, Kate didn't think she'd ever get used to the fact that it rained in the middle of summer and the temperature didn't go down even a degree. Ninety degrees and ninety percent humidity was a tough adjustment to make after living in Southern California's dry desert heat.

But then she was finding it hard to adjust to almost everything about this move. She just didn't feel like adjusting, she admitted to herself as she eased her car into her parking space. She stared at the concrete wall in front of her, making no effort to get out, though with the engine off, the air conditioning vanished and the car almost immediately became a steam bath.

It wasn't that there was anything wrong with New Jersey. At least, there was nothing wrong with it that wouldn't have also been wrong with any of the other forty-nine states.

Drew.

She closed her eyes against the pain in her chest. There didn't seem to be much reason to adapt to the new life that had been provided for her, not when she felt dead inside. The only thing that made it possible for her to keep going was the knowledge that he was all right, that he'd survived the shooting and was going to make a full recovery.

Sighing, she got out of the car and pulled the bag of groceries from the passenger seat. Wrapping her arm around it, she made her way up the steps to the first level of apartments. Her apartment was at the far end from the garage and she supposed it would make a miserable trip when winter came. The thought didn't bother her.

Sooner or later, she'd surely snap out of this depression. After all, she had a lot to be grateful for. Lester Davis was in prison, serving a lengthy term as a result of her testimony as well as that of one of the gunmen he'd hired to kill her. She'd been given refuge by the Witness Protection Program. She had a new identity, a new job and a new life in a new city. Drew was alive and healthy somewhere.

And probably well on his way to forgetting her, she thought bleakly. Maybe she'd only imagined him saying that he loved her. In the stress of the moment, she could have imagined almost anything. And it didn't really matter, anyway. Even if he did love her, it didn't change the situation, which was that he had a life, a job, a career. And he couldn't have any of those things with her. Not anymore.

Her own life was on hold. In a way, she felt as if she was just marking time, waiting for Davis's men to find her, waiting to become a news story, like poor Joseph Smithson. She shook her head and pushed away the morbid thought. She was alive and she'd been given a chance to build a new life. She had to be grateful for that. And if that new life seemed like an empty shell without Drew, then she was just going to have to learn to live with it.

Blinking back tears, she hefted the bag a little higher on her hip and struggled to find her key. She fitted it into the lock and shoved the door open, sighing as she stepped into the air-conditioned comfort of her apartment. She didn't bother to switch on any lights, relying on the muted illumination of sunlight through the drapes as she made her way to the kitchen.

She'd just set the bag on the counter when she heard someone speak her name.

"Kate."

She froze, feeling as if she'd fallen through a time warp. A few months ago, another state, another apartment. The same voice. Only he'd called her Ms. Sloane then. She closed her eyes for a minute, telling herself that she was hallucinating. She'd spent too many lonely nights lying awake fantasizing about Drew finding her. Afraid of having the charade that was her life found out, she'd isolated herself, living in her memories. That's all it was.

"Kate." She shuddered and closed her eyes, feeling as if her sanity hung by the thinnest of threads. "Look at me, Kate." There was tenderness in that impossible voice.

"No."

"Why not?"

"Because I've imagined you too many times. And always, when I open my eyes, you're not there. I don't think I could bear it again."

There was a whisper of movement behind her and then she felt hands close over her arms, strong and hard. And real. He turned her to face him but she kept her eyes shut, childishly afraid to open them.

"Look at me, Kate. I'm really here this time."

Hesitantly she lifted her eyelids and stared into Drew's familiar ice blue eyes. He looked just as she remembered him. Thinner, maybe, with new hollows under his cheekbones, evidence of how close he'd come to dying, of how long and hard the recovery had been.

"Drew?" She lifted her fingers to his face, needing to feel the reality of him. "You're here."

"I'm here. I came as soon as I could. You didn't think you'd get rid of me that easily, did you?"

"I didn't know. I wasn't sure you didn't want to be gotten rid of."

The tangled sentence made him cock one eyebrow, his mouth quirking with humor.

"I didn't want to be gotten rid of," he told her. His hands slid from her shoulders to her back, pulling her closer. "I don't plan on ever being gotten rid of."

"How did you find me?"

"By twisting a lot of arms, calling in every favor I was ever owed and breaking the law half a dozen times. I love you."

They were the words she'd dreamed of hearing. She closed her eyes, savoring them, even as she knew she had to send him away.

"You can't love me."

"Why not? Because I was too stupid to admit it before this?"

"It's not that." She twisted out of his arms, backing a few steps away, knowing she had to rush the words out now, before she let her hunger for him drown out her common sense.

"I'm in the witness program, Drew."

"I know that. Why do you think it took me so long to track you down? I wouldn't have been able to find you if Lavery hadn't been willing to pull a few strings for me." He smiled and reached for her, but she edged away.

"I have a new identity. A whole new life."

"I know what the witness program is, Kate." His smile had faded, his eyes taking on a wary look. Was it too late? Was there no place for him in this new life?

"Then you know I can't go back to L.A. Not as long as Davis is alive."

"I'm not asking you to go back." He reached out and caught her hands, drawing her forward, despite her halfhearted resistance. "I'm staying here."

"You can't. You've got a life in California. A job. Friends."

"I don't have a life without you." He wrapped his arms around her, holding her close, feeling relief wash over him. She was trying to send him away for his own sake. "If you have to make a new life, we'll make it together. There's nothing in California that I can't live without. But I can't live without you."

She hesitated, torn between her need to believe him and her fear that he'd come to regret his decision.

"You can't give up everything for me."

"I already have."

"You'll end up hating me," she whispered.

"Not in this lifetime." He caught her hand, putting it against his heart. "It took me a long time to admit it, but I need you, Kate. I love you and I need you in my life. Don't ask me to leave."

"I should."

"What does your heart say, Kate? What does it tell you to do?"

She closed her eyes, knowing she was about to take the biggest chance of her lifetime. When she opened them again, they were almost pure green and filled with love.

"My heart says I'd be a fool to try and get rid of you."

"Listen to it, Kate." His mouth was only a whisper away from hers. "Listen to your heart."

As if she could do anything else, Kate thought, lifting her arms to draw him close.

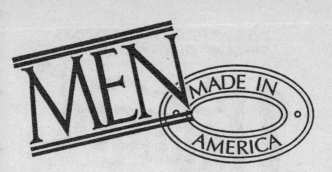

MEN MADE IN AMERICA

Fifty red-blooded, white-hot, true-blue hunks from every State in the Union!

Beginning in May, look for MEN MADE IN AMERICA! Written by some of our most popular authors, these stories feature fifty of the strongest, sexiest men, each from a different state in the union!

Two titles available every other month at your favorite retail outlet.

In May, look for:

FULL HOUSE by Jackie Weger (Alabama)
BORROWED DREAMS by Debbie Macomber (Alaska)

In July, look for:

CALL IT DESTINY by Jayne Ann Krentz (Arizona)
ANOTHER KIND OF LOVE by Mary Lynn Baxter (Arkansas)

You won't be able to resist MEN MADE IN AMERICA!

THREE UNFORGETTABLE HEROINES
THREE AWARD-WINNING AUTHORS

Untamed

MAVERICK HEARTS

A unique collection of historical short stories that capture the spirit of America's last frontier.

HEATHER GRAHAM POZZESSERE—over 10 million copies of her books in print worldwide
Lonesome Rider—The story of an Eastern widow and the renegade half-breed who becomes her protector.

PATRICIA POTTER—an author whose books are consistently Waldenbooks bestsellers
Against the Wind—Two people, battered by heartache, prove that love can heal all.

JOAN JOHNSTON—award-winning Western historical author with 17 books to her credit
One Simple Wish—A woman with a past discovers that dreams really do come true.

Join us for an exciting journey West with
UNTAMED
Available in July, wherever Harlequin books are sold.

MAV93

Harlequin is proud to present our
best authors and their best books.
Always the best for your reading
pleasure!

Throughout 1993, Harlequin will bring you
exciting books by some of the top names in
contemporary romance!

In June,
look for
*Threats and
Promises* by

BARBARA
DELINSKY

The plan was to make her nervous....

Lauren Stevens was so preoccupied with her new looks
and her new business that she really didn't notice a
pattern to the peculiar "little incidents"—incidents
that could eventually take her life. However, she did
notice the sudden appearance of the attractive and
interesting Matt Kruger who *claimed* to be a close
friend of her dead brother....

Find out more in THREATS AND
PROMISES...available wherever Harlequin
books are sold.